THE NIGHT CHICAGO DIED AND OTHER STORIES

Tom Wessex

authorHOUSE®

AuthorHouse™
1663 Liberty Drive, Suite 200
Bloomington, IN 47403
www.authorhouse.com
Phone: 1-800-839-8640

This book is a work of fiction. People, places, events, and situations are the product of the author's imagination. Any resemblance to actual persons, living or dead, or historical events, is purely coincidental.

First published by AuthorHouse 7/15/2008

ISBN: 978-1-4389-0011-7 (sc)

Printed in the United States of America
Bloomington, Indiana

This book is printed on acid-free paper.

Table of Contents

The Night Chicago Died

"Where were you the night Chicago died?" asked the pale man in a serge suit who stood threateningly over me. His eyes were hidden by dark sun glasses.

"I don't know any Chicago," I replied. I looked down at the table at which I was seated. I still remember the wood's patina.

The pale man walked to the corner of the interview room's lone window. He was tall and lank. The serge suit seemed to hang on him as if he were a scarecrow. He looked out the window, and I could not see his face as he repeated the question.

"Where were you the night Chicago died?"

This time I chose not to respond, searching the wood of the table in front of me as I wondered about a way to escape.

The black grooves melted into knots and I crossed my eyes to heighten the effect. Out of my left eye, a face formed in the wood. The many years of varnish had rendered certain areas black. I looked more closely and sure enough it was a face, the face of Chicago.

I had known Chicago since childhood; he was two years older than I and had been a playmate of my brother's'. We had grown up in the tough housing projects around Ninth Street, both the product of single mothers, our fathers long dead.

Life was tough and we matured quickly, no time for school or fun we went straight into the crime ridden streets. Chicago made a name for himself as an enforcer and I as a drug runner. Both of us had survival instincts befitting of our upbringings and within several years had made it the top of our professions.

Our paths crossed infrequently over the next few years. I did a small stint in jail and Chicago moved out west to take care of some business. Now and then I would catch sight of him in a bar or on a corner. I would wave or call a greeting and he always acknowledged me.

Sometime in '97 new faces showed up in our neighborhood, tough reformed criminals who had found Islam. The streets started to clean up and business became difficult. The Muslims were well organized and equipped and street hustlers like us were no match for them. Our former customers now packed the mosques and we all headed out of town to pursue our interest elsewhere.

Later that year in small bar in a western town I bumped into Chicago. He seemed happy and talked at length about how his life had changed for the better. Gone were his enforcing days, he had now made it to the top. Directly supplied by some Italians back east he was running his own game, less hassle was how he described it. No more late nights.

I admitted to him it sounded inviting and he said he needed a good man and although we had never been in the same outfits, we had known each other since youth. He needed a man he could trust.

"You don't know Chicago?" said the pale man in the serge suit. "You guys grew up together." The man laughed. He knew I was lying.

"Tell me," he said, "what do you see when you look into that table top?"

"Nothing," I replied.

The pale man walked away from the window. Thrusting his hands in his pockets, he looked directly at me. I did not like the attention.

"Why you lookin' at me like that?" I asked.

The pale man did not answer the question. He asked another.
"Okay. Let's try this. Where were you last night?"
"At home," I answered.
"With whom?" asked the pale man?
"Alone," I answered.

The pale man took off his serge jacket and hung it on the back of the chair opposite me. I remember thinking that the jacket hung on the chair back better than it did on him. Then sitting down in front of me, he offered me a cigarette.

I accepted and he lit one for me and himself. The smoke eased my nerves somewhat and I smiled at the pale man. He did not smile back; resting his half smoked cigarette in the ashtray he stood up again and walked to the window.

"I'm going to ask you again," he said. "Where were you the night Chicago died?"

The room was still, a thin line of smoke rose vertically from his cigarette toward the ceiling. About a foot in the air the line broke and dispersed. Looking into this dispersing smoke I fancied I saw images, first a cloud, then an ice cream and finally a face. The face was Chicago's.

Chicago had misled me. He had no new job, no new business and no Italians supplying him. When he took me back to his apartment, I should have known. He now lived in a trendy part of town and his apartment was a decent size.

When I arrived at the complex door I had to buzz Chicago to let me in, he did and I took the elevator up to his apartment on the third floor.

Opening the front door he let me in. I walked down a long tiled hallway to a living room area.

He offered me a cigarette and I watched him through the veil of smoke when he exhaled.

The apartment was decorated in a decidedly middle-eastern style. The rugs were beautifully sewn, the images of camels hand woven. On the coffee table near where we were seated lay several copies of the Koran.

"Sit down man," said Chicago jovially. "Make yourself at home."

"What's this, man?" I asked, pointing at the Koran.
"This is the truth, man," he answered with a smile.
I laughed out loud.
"Come off it, man," I said. "Have you lost it?"
"Yeah, I've lost it," he replied. "Lost all that foolish stuff I used to do."
"I ain't in for religion," I said.
"I know that," said Chicago. "But I got to try." He grinned.
"Well you tried, man," I said. "Now, I'm outta here. Man, keep this stuff to you."
Chicago nodded and we finished our cigarettes. He asked about some of my relatives and me about his. Before I left he wished me well and hugged me.

The pale man spoke at the window again.
"I need to know what happened the night Chicago died."
"Listen, man," I said. "I don't know what you talkin' about."
Turning around the man walked over and sat down again. He stared directly at men. The reflection in his sunglasses was not me but Chicago.
"Chicago was going to kill you that night," he said.

The night Chicago died I met him by chance outside a movie theatre in town. It was a bustling affair. I do not remember the name of the movie I saw. Chicago had company and, greeting me enthusiastically, he asked. "Man, did you come over to work with me yet?"
"No," I replied.
His face became more somber. He said that it upset him. Taking me to one side, he leaned against a poster board. He wanted me to come with him. It was a rough world out there. People wished me harm.
"Who?" I asked.
"People," he replied.

4

"Who are they?" I asked. It is always wise to know who is after you.

"Me," replied Chicago. Then lowering his voice he told me that some people at the local mosque viewed me as a danger to the neighborhood and they had given go ahead to remove me in the name of neighborhood cleanliness. He added that he had been instructed to carry out the deed soon.

This was serious.

"So," continued the pale man. "Now do you want to try again? Where were you the night Chicago died?"

"I was here," I replied.

Standing up again, the pale man slammed his clenched fist on the table. The table rocked momentarily. The pale man kept his fist clenched and showed no sign of pain.

"You are lying to me," he said. "No one saw you here."

To argue with him was fruitless, and I knew it. He walked around the table like a tiger ready to pounce. The room was getting warmer too; beads of sweat broke out on his brow. He loosened his tie and left the room.

I was left alone in the stuffy room with nothing to drink. Turning round in my chair I yelled in the direction of the door.

"It's warm in here. Can I get a drink or something"?

No one replied but the ceiling fan began to slowly turn. I looked at it carefully. A moving fan can play many tricks with the mind, and watching the circular motion my mind wandered. I had seen the fan's motion somewhere before. Now I remembered, there was a ceiling fan in the apartment the night Chicago died.

Chicago's apartment was not the place to kill a man. It was so homely and comfortable looking that I almost had second thoughts. Chicago had buzzed me in and I made my way up to his apartment.

After exchanging pleasantries he looked at me deeply, his round face seeming lost in the surroundings. I imagined him momentarily as a sage sat dispensing wisdom to the people of our old neighborhood. Gone were the frown lines of his youth, Chicago was all smiles and I realized I preferred him with a smile on his face.

He lit a cigarette and watching the exhaled smoke rise he turned to me and asked.

"You wouldn't deny a condemned man a last smoke."

I was a little taken aback by the comment and also suspicious. Had someone tipped Chicago off? I reached for my weapon and covered him. He smiled.

"What you laughing at man? I'm gonna put a cap in you."

"I want a last request," he said.

"Go ahead," I said motioning with my weapon.

"That after you've plugged me, you at least bring the news to the masjid." He sounded so sincere when he said it that momentarily I contemplated it.

"What you think I'm mad man. I ain't going near that place." I yelled, thinking better of it after the fact.

"Okay, deny me then, we been knowing each other a long time," said Chicago. If he was nervous, I did not detect it in his voice.

I do not remember when I finally decided to shoot Chicago. But I did. I hit him twice in the middle of the chest. He died on the couch with the same big grin on his face. As his blood soaked into his white shirt I thought I made out a form in it. Looking again I nearly jumped out of my skin. The pattern of the blood had formed in the shape of Chicago's face.

I sat staring at it for a long time. For some reason my eyes would not leave it. I had to drag myself out of its hypnotic gaze. When I did, I closed Chicago's eyes and walked out of the apartment.

The pale man in the serge suit returned with a glass of water for me.

"I don't know whether you deserve this or not," he said. "But, here you are."

The water was cool and I drank it all and asked for more. The man in the pale suit held up his hand as if to tell me no. Then sitting on the edge of the table, one foot on the floor, he asked me again,

"Where were you the night Chicago died?"

The water had taken its effect. My mouth, once dry, was now wet and moist. The cigarette had relaxed me. I stared back at the pale man.

"Alright, I saw Chicago the night he died, outside a movie theatre downtown. Chicago was drunk."

The pale man raised his eyebrows.

"Chicago was drunk the night he died?"

"Yes, Sir," I replied.

The man in the pale suit offered me another cigarette. This time the brand was different. Menthol, my favorite. I eagerly took one and the pale man lit it for me. I drew deeply on my cigarette.

"How did you know Chicago was drunk?" he asked his sunglass eyes unmoving.

"Listen, man," I started.

"Don't call me man," the pale man said. I knew he meant it.

"I mean I know the smell of alcohol," I rephrased my answer.

The door opened and another man short and muscular entered the room with another glass of water for me.

Setting it down on the table the short man glared at and said. "Don't touch that water man until the man says you can."

The glass of water looked inviting sat on the table. I wondered if I could snatch it quick and drink it before the pale man could stop me. Too risky, I reasoned. Better sit tight.

"Now," said the pale man. He moved the glass of water right in front of me. I gazed down into the glass and watched the still water. My face reflected out at me. I looked cruel. I recognized the expression; it was the same expression I saw in the mirror in my room the night Chicago died.

Making my way through the crowded streets of town I fancied I saw Chicago's face a thousand times. On every street I stopped and turned around at least once. Was Chicago following me or was I imagining things. Arriving back my room, I sat down on my bed, relieved to be alone. On my wall was a mirror. I forget where I bought it, or if I'd ever looked in it.

Standing up I looked in the mirror and was shocked at what I saw. It must have been some years since I looked at my own reflection. I looked cruel and drawn. This was not how I remembered my self, how I saw myself, as walked the streets, as I greeted people or as I had sat opposite Chicago that evening.

My adrenalin was running so hard that I needed calming down. I thought of everything. I took a drink, I took a smoke and I even smoked a joint. Nothing would calm me. Lying on my bed I closed my eyes. Trying to drive the thoughts of my face out of my mind I imagined myself as a child. I stood in the stairwell of the project where I grew up. I was waiting for someone to meet me. I heard footsteps, and then I saw Chicago.

The pale man told me to drink my water.

"Telling the truth can be a thirsty pastime," he said with a touch of sarcasm to his voice.

I drank the water, a long cool drink. It was very satisfying.

"Yeah, Chicago was drunk," I said. "And he tried to kill me."

The pale man said that he knew Chicago was going to kill me, but Chicago was dead and he wanted to know why and at whose hand. He started again.

"You knew Chicago. You met him on the stairs two floors down from your mother's apartment."

I said nothing.

"You knew Chicago from that day on," he continued. "He didn't want kill you. I don't know why not, but he didn't want to do it."

I still said nothing.

The pale man got off the table and walked over to the window. He seemed oblivious to me staring out of the window. He continued talking.

"You met him that day, and you killed him that night. You pumped two bullets into his chest. You washed up in his kitchen. You wiped your hands on his towel. You were there the night Chicago died."

He pointed a long bony finger at me.

I shook my head, but the pale man continued, the volume of his voice rising.

"You walked home, your usual route. You walked quickly. You did not have the time of day for anyone. You fell asleep on your bed and you woke up here."

Momentarily I lost my senses and fell for the bait.

"How do you know all this?" I asked

"Because," the pale man said, putting on his jacket and scooping up his pack of cigarettes, "I was there the night Chicago died."

Albert, Max and the Wonderful New Toy Train Set

Albert's father was fond of saying, "Only by acknowledging our own irrationalities can we achieve rationality."

His son was not so sure, but he went along with them all the same. Albert lived with his parents in an apartment on a secluded street in Munich. The buildings were dour and grey, built in early gothic style; they boasted several mean looking gargoyles underneath the soffit.

The monstrous statuettes had given Albert nightmares as a small child. He had resolved these problems, at age five when, his father bought him a compass for his birthday. It was made of shiny brass, and Albert had spent hours studying it, finally vanishing his demons into an imaginary substance in which the needle moved. He called this substance first ether and later space.

Today was Albert's birthday again, and he eagerly awaited the return of his father who had been attending an exhibition in Leipzig for the last three days. Albert had hoped to accompany him there, but his age had precluded it. All that being said, he hoped his father had bought him a birthday gift from the exhibition. Albert knew only the newest and most technical of toys were on sale at the exhibition, and he had spent hours leafing through a brochure his father had shown him.

Arriving home that day, Albert put his school satchel down and kissed his mother. She tutted at his messy hair. However she may try, her son's hair could not be tamed; it stood on his head like a spiked bush.

His mother had prepared a spread of fish dishes, pastries and cake to serve as a birthday meal for Albert and welcome home for her husband. The party was to begin the moment Albert's father crossed the threshold. Also invited was Albert's cousin Max. Albert loved his cousin Max. He was the older brother he never had and the two spent considerable time together. Max was sixteen and a Talmud scholar. He was very religious, and Albert, though he disagreed with him on most points was careful not to offend him.

Albert ran to his room barely containing his excitement at his father's pending arrival, his mother's voice in the background urged him not to run, but he was not listening.

Albert's room was small, but contained one large window through which he could look out into the street below. His school clothes were tight and rigid as was normal in those days, and Albert hurriedly changed, tossing his clothes into a pile in the corner of his room.

As he was dressing in his casual clothes his eyes rarely left the window, hoping to catch a glimpse of his father as he walked into the building. Albert's father knew his son watched for his return, and the two would engage in long face-pulling antics from window to street, much to the chagrin of his mother.

Today however, to add a larger element of surprise, Albert's father had taken the rear entrance to the building. After sometime waiting by the window, Albert walked back into the living room dejected.

What a sight beheld him. His mother had neatly decorated the dining room table with food. There were biscuits, sandwiches and other assorted delights. Albert cheered up immediately and gave his mother a big hug, sneaking a small biscuit from the pile his mother had neatly arranged on a silver plate.

Presently there was a knock at the front door to the apartment, and Albert's father entered the room. He was a stocky, kindly looking fellow and he loved his son more than anything in the world, although truth be told he had always worried about him. Albert appeared slow to his father and at times extremely self-absorbed.

In one hand Albert's father held his cane and gloves and under the other arm carried a wrapped gift. Albert, beaming, ran to meet his father pulling him over to the dining room table, where he showed him the spread his mother had prepared, which now included a large iced cake. His father grinned at the spread and removed his hat, telling Albert to go and hang it up for him.

Albert returned to his side, and his father tousled his unkempt hair.

"Happy birthday, son." he said. "I have a little something for you."

He had a glint in his eye and tone in voice that laid an inference on his pleasure at purchasing the gift.

"Can I have it now please?" pleaded Albert, his eyes looking imploringly at his father.

"Is Max here yet?" inquired his father.

No sooner had he spoken, than there was another knock at the door. Albert opened it and in walked Max.

Max was a tall youth with a happy go lucky grin and a mop of black hair. Max too had brought a present for Albert. The two cousins hugged and joined Albert's parents in the dining room.

"And now," said Albert's father slowly and deliberately, "here is a little something I picked up in Leipzig." He handed Albert a large package wrapped in gift paper.

Albert opened his gift eagerly, carelessly discarding the wrapping paper on the floor. When the wrapping paper was off, a new Macklin toy train set was revealed. It was the latest model of its kind, boasting an engine, tender and two sleeping cars. It came complete with a length of track and small wooden stationhouse. Young Albert who could barely contain his excitement, managed to hug his father.

"Can we build it right now Papa?" he asked his face the epitome of joy.

"Once we have eaten, dear boy," answered his father, laughing. He, too, was secretly excited about the toy.

Max, Albert and his father sat themselves around the table; they were soon joined by his mother. She removed her apron and started to serve the boys. The birthday meal was over quickly. Most of the conversation centered on inquiries into Albert's progress at school and his father's experiences in Leipzig.

When everyone had got down from the table, Albert's mother began clearing the plates away while the two cousins got to work assembling the new toy train set. Opening the box, they laid the track out on the living room floor. Max interlocked the pieces of rail, and Albert placed the engine on the track.

The engine was a wind-up. Albert took the key provided and wound up the engine and delicately placed it back on the track. Toys in those days were very basic and the engine slowly moved down the track as the spindle unwound. Several times it derailed, and Albert spent some time resetting it on the rails.

Like most inquisitive children, Albert started almost immediately to experiment. He soon coupled the tender and train cars to his engine. The addition of the extra pieces, however, slowed the engine further. Albert was looking for speed, his young mind working overtime on how to make his engine go faster.

Albert and Max decided to raise one end of the track on wooden blocks in an attempt to increase the speed. This, however, was not successful; the downward acceleration was greater than the speed produced by the unwinding of the windlass. Added to this, the persistent winding had put a strain on the windlass, and the constant activity had caused the rails to separate from each other in several places. The two boys again rebuilt the track, although this time Albert removed all but the straight rails.

Once the track was back together Albert raised the engine's starting point several inches more trying to increase its speed. When this failed he raised it higher and then higher still. The elevation however did not give him the desired result.

Eventually Max suggested that they disengage the axles from the winding system. Albert thought it a great idea, but worried his father would be angry. The train after all had been a birthday present and an expensive one at that.

Looking closely at the under carriage of the engine, Max noticed that the heads of the small screws holding the windlass could possibly be turned with a kitchen knife, so he crept into the kitchen and took out the utensil.

The boys made short work of the axles which soon lay in pieces on the floor. Once again, they started raising one end of the track.

Urging Max to roll the train from even greater heights, Albert's mind began wandering. Max, tired of his little cousin's exortions, balanced the end of the track carefully on seat of an old armchair some two feet off the floor. Without turning round he released the engine.

Albert laid waiting and thinking on the floor, his head positioned directly in front of the end of the track. Gazing along the length of the track, he saw Max release the engine. The action seemed very remote to Albert and appeared to be happening in slow-motion.

The next three seconds seemed like an eternity to Albert as he watched the engine's progress as if outside the sphere of being. As the toy engine accelerated toward him, Albert watched in comfort from the floor as it grew in size. Albert found himself looking closely at the detail on the front end of his toy, with all the time in the world to move if he wanted to. As the giant engine got closer, he imagined himself lying across a full-sized track as the ever-enlarging toy closed in on him and struck him on the nose.

His cousin Max watched with horror as the engine shot down the track and within an instant hit his little cousin on the nose, before he could move to intercept it.

All Albert got out of that afternoon was a scratched nose and a scolding from his father, who had to spend sometime rebuilding the wheel train on his son's present. Later that night in bed Albert lay thinking. It was as if a whole new world had been opened to him.....

Many years later in his study in Princeton, Albert, surrounded by books, related the story of the toy train to me. He said he had kept it secret all these years, and if asked the origins of the theories which had changed the world, he instead told a tale about a railway track and some flags he had experimented with in Switzerland in his twenties.

"This story," he said. "is consigned to eternity with me."

Captain Falkenberg's Gambit

Captain Falkenberg of the Dutch East India Company was a noted mariner, twenty times rounding the Cape of Good Hope and with a resume that most masters would die for. Now his thirty years on the high seas were coming to an end and his craggy wind burnt face carried a look of despondency. For Falkenberg knew no other home than the sea and any land ties he may have had were long extinguished. Often he fancied committing suicide and spent long nights conjuring up the most humane and least painful way to end his life experience.

Frequent trips along the same passage had allowed boredom to set in, and Captain Falkenberg had put the idle hours to good use, devising a new chess gambit. A stealthy attack against one's opponents Queen's side. This gambit, he conjectured, would make him almost infallible on the chessboard.

This particular trip, Captain Falkenberg's ship had rounded the Cape of Good Hope and made good speed to the Indies and now, returning, her hold laden with nutmeg and mace she was hugging the coastline off Cape Agulhas. The weather had been fair and Falkenberg delegated his duties to the first officer so he could spend most of his time on the aft deck staring out to sea, a distant look in his eyes.

The crew hoping for a shoring in Cape Town had diligently attended their duties and as the evening approached the conversation on board was of the beauty of Hottentot women and the smoothness of Cape wines.

Captain Falkenberg did not care for his crew. They were lowland Hollanders, mistrusting of Germans and they let him know it at every opportunity. That being the case the Captain chose to keep to his quarters or his seat on the aft deck.

Falkenberg's ship a handsome square rigger called the "Fliegen Hollander," and it was a pleasure to sail. Easy to handle, good at close maneuvering and with all modern conveniences, she was the pride of the Dutch East India Company's fleet.

Falkenberg had spent most of the morning walking the decks, monitoring his vessel's condition.

The late afternoon rolled in that day with only high clouds and a quartering sea to report. Captain Falkenberg kept his usual station near the helm, his gaze on the horizon.

Squalls are rare that time of year in the Southern Atlantic; any rough weather is normally related to the meeting of the oceans off Cape Agulhas. As the ship plied across the point, the clouds thickened, skies darkened significantly, and the crew trimmed the sails. The keen south-east breeze picked up to a gale, and the ship starting to heave to leeward. The conditions, although not treacherous, caused precautionary measures to be taken and the mate called all none essential crew below. Captain Falkenberg, however, remained seated, gazing out to sea, behind him the helmsman, a tall wizened Dutchman, hands on the wheel, was the only other man on deck.

The second officer was a young Dutchman with a round, baby face. He was given the job of advising the Captain to retire to quarters until the squall passed. Wobbling slightly from the ships instability he stood behind Falkenberg and informed him of the situation. The Captain was a large man rugged and weather beaten. He did not mince his words and without turning around told the young Dutchman he would be down presently.

"Aye, Aye." replied the young Dutchman. "I should advise you though, Captain, that this is not an evening one should linger above deck." This time his voice lingered momentarily on the wind.

Captain Falkenberg's head shot round at the sound of the Dutchman's voice. A glint of recognition passed over his face. He eyed the young man in the navy blue jacket and britches.

"How old are you lad?" He inquired.

"I'm eighteen," The Dutchman replied. His pale blue butcher's eyes mirroring the Captains stare.

"That's young," said Captain Falkenberg, a tinge of sadness in his voice. The vessel listed slightly to port as he spoke. The young Dutchman stumbled and regained his footing. Falkenberg however remained virtually motionless his body seeming to flow with the tossed ship.

"Do you play chess?" inquired Captain Falkenberg.

"Not well," admitted the Dutchman.

"Damn you man," yelled the Captain rising from his chair he pushed his face directly at the young Dutchman. "Answer me directly man. That's an order."

If the Dutchman was scared he certainly did not show it. He simply nodded his head in assent and said, "Yes sir, I can play, although I haven't played in an eternity."

Captain Falkenberg did not move, remaining deep in thought as if he was trying to recall something. Snapping out of a momentary daze spoke sharply to the young Dutchman.

"Then fetch the board, and let's play before it darkens for good." Falkenberg spoke with the confidence knowing his instruction would be followed. He sat back down, and resumed his study of the shortening horizon.

The young Dutchman took his leave of the Captain and headed below, casting an uneasy eye to the skies.

The ship rocked and rolled in the high seas, but still the helmsman held her steady. Falkenberg remained at his station and sat down on the chair gazing out at the white caps. If there was any change in him it was not visible.

After a short while another man appeared on deck next to Falkenberg. This fellow was older, although also Dutch, his insignia indicated he was the first mate. In his right hand he held an unlighted sea lamp and in the other a box.

"Evening sir, steady as she goes?" The first mate had a nasal twang to his voice,

Falkenberg spun around at the sound of the voice; he eyed his new companion up and down and nodded to himself.

"It's you," he replied. "Don't you goddamn people ever stop creeping up on each other?"

The first mate smiled. "You should at least be used to it by now sir," he said.

"Used, yes," replied Falkenberg, gazing at the stormy seas. "But I don't have to like it."

The advent of the squall had darkened the skies sufficiently that the lamp was now needed. The first mate lit it with his tinder box and placed it beside the Captain.

"Put that infernal thing out." roared Falkenberg squinting in its light.

"I cannot," replied the first mate, "you know the rules Captain."

"Why can't you damn people do as you are told?" asked Falkenberg. "I've never met a Dutchman worth a shit."

The Dutchman did not react his face motionless as if used to the insult. The skies had darkened further with the onset of twilight. The helmsman requested refreshment and lights for the bow.

"Hold your damn course," barked Falkenberg look for the False bay beacon," and stood up as if meaning to back his comments up.

The Helmsman looked over uneasily at the Captain. Falkenberg could see the whites of his knuckles as they clutched the wheel. The vessel pulled and rolled, but still the Helmsman held her steady.

"Well sir?" asked the first mate as if ignoring the Captain's previous order.

"What are your orders?" he asked again, the lighted lamp mooning his demonic face.

Falkenberg momentarily held his face in his hand. Then drawing his palm the length of his face, he groaned.

"The same." said Falkenberg solemnly. "Stay the course. We shall cross False Bay shortly."

"Shall we play?" asked the first mate

"I prefer the dice," said Falkenberg wryly adjusting his chair to face his first officer.

"Set the damn pieces up and then get me a drink." ordered Captain Falkenberg

"As you wish sir." replied the first mate, and he proceeded to set the board up. The constant rocking had no effect upon the tiny figures; they remained motionless on their spaces. When finished he tipped his cap, and headed back below leaving the lamp behind.

Falkenberg stared at the chessmen as if looking through them; his hard brown face began to sneer. Nervously he pulled on his graying beard. The sky outside was nearly dark and the lamp shone clear and true its gaze resting idly on the Captain's wrinkled brow.

The Helmsman locked the wheel on course and sat down opposite the Captain.

"Your move sir," he said coldly.

"Get to your post, you damn Dutch fool," screamed Falkenberg, he got up to make toward the helm, but the helmsman grabbed his arm and held it tightly. So tight was the grip that the Captain winced. The helmsman spoke.

"It's alright sir, we're on course." he said. The words seemed to reassure Falkenberg and he sat down again.

"I cannot see the Cape Point beacon." said Falkenberg, a touch of anxiety in his voice. "We should have sighted it by now, and where's that other damn fool?"

"Your move sir," said the helmsman, pulling his cap further over his eyes.

"Damn you people," the Captain muttered under his breath. "Always the same. Hurry, hurry."

The sea lamp shone brightly on the two adversaries, lighting the faces of Falkenberg and his Helmsman, but neither looked up both engrossed in the game before them. On the bow, the ship plied toward the point, waves breaking across the fo'csle.

Eventually, after a rapid exchange of pieces, Falkenberg grinned thinking victory was in his grasp. On his lips he could taste the salty air.

The helmsman opposite him was deep in thought. The wind had picked up to a strong gale, and his hair was blown in his face. His eyes cut the night like blue daggers as he reasoned his next move.

"It appears you are in trouble," said Falkenberg arrogantly, sitting back in his chair as he spoke. "My gambit has worked. All you goddamn people are stupid. I always knew it."

The helmsman raised his head, stared coldly at the Captain and said, "The night is long, Captain Falkenberg."

"Not long enough," snapped Falkenberg in reply. "You are beaten at last. Look, I see the beacon at Cape Point off the bow, hard to starboard, Dutchman, for Table bay." Captain Falkenberg seemed excited at their impending approach.

"I need to make my move first, Sir." replied the Helmsman.

"Well, god dammit, make it," said the Captain. "That's an order."

When the helmsman hesitated, Captain Falkenberg got up again and started to shout.

"The game is won, back to the wheel Dutchman, hard to starboard for Table Bay. Let's get off this godforsaken ship."

"I have to take my move, Sir." replied the Helmsman.

"Resign, you've lost," snapped Falkenberg.

"I must move, for you cannot cheat me, Captain." The Helmsman's eyes did not look up as he spoke. The rigging creaked ominously, and the wind whistled through the sails. The Cape point beacon shed an eerie light over the bow.

Falkenberg leapt from his chair and lunged toward the wheel. His leg brushed the lamp, which tumbled over and extinguished itself quickly, leaving the Captain stumbling in the dark and cursing.

"I won dammit, I won." he yelled into the night but no one replied. The night was silent.

The trip back from the Indies had been a good one for Captain Falkenberg. His ship had made good speed and he sat on the aft deck contemplating his impending retirement. The sound of a voice made him turn. He thought he had heard the voice someplace before. Behind him stood a young Dutchman no more than eighteen years of age.......

An Afternoon on Skull Hill

Should a man be held accountable if he willing sacrifices himself to save another? Or if he saves a person while condemning another? These are profound questions, both moral and philosophical.

In these times such answers are only reachable in places of learning, it was no different centuries ago......

The fifth procurator of Judea, a tall well-built man with aquiline features and a slightly balding head had established such a place of learning in Caesarea Maritime. Under his auspices, it had flourished and become somewhat renowned. It was built in a Doric style boasting many fine colonnades and an exquisitely kept garden.

The procurator, whose name was Pontius Pilate, although he had been a soldier and administrator these last twenty years, had earlier in his life been a scholar of some standing. He had several notable orations to his name. By nature he was considered somewhat of a humanist.

One of the procurator's favorite pastimes was to leisurely stroll along the upper levels of the library and gaze out of the windows into the vastness of the Mediterranean Sea. Pilate had been born on the rough shores of Calabria, and the water held a special significance for him.

On these strolls he oft times took one young librarian in his employ, tutoring him in subjects on which he was an authority. The librarian, named Gestas, was from Zor, his heritage unknown but having the same keen features evident on his employer's countenance.

The procurator had a soft spot for the youth and spent many long hours in his company discussing the nature of truth. Both had developed a healthy respect for the other's cognitive powers.

On this particular morning, their conversation had taken a decidedly personnel turn. Walking along the western balcony of the library so Pilate could view his beloved Mediterranean, the two had started to discuss the issue of the young man's heritage. It was a warm spring morning and a pleasant breeze was drifting in off the sea.

"I have been informed," started Gestas nervously in Greek. "that you are my father hegemon."

The procurator of Judea had spent a lifetime perfecting the art of looking surprised. Today was no different and he did so with some skill. He raised his dark eyebrows and stared quizzically at his young companion.

If Gestas was expecting a reply, he was going to be disappointed. Pilate had learned many years previously not to respond to searching questions.

"Well," said Gestas, with a touch of insolence in his voice, "will you not at least deny it?"

The procurator of Judea trained his glance on the distant sea, as if looking beyond it toward Rome itself. His eyes closed briefly as if trying to recall something.

"Consider it denied," he said after some time.

Gestas looked at the man stood opposite him, for the first time he became aware of distinct likeness between himself and his employer. "Is that your final position?" he asked.

Pilate's all-knowing stare answered it for him. He swept his toga across his body and left the young man alone on the balcony.

Later that night, maybe feeling guilty, the procurator left his residence and headed over to the library. The effects of several mugs of Falernian running through his head, he wished to speak to Gestas. He was disappointed, however, to find that the young man had left abruptly that afternoon, leaving no timetable for his return.

Some years hence on a similar morning, Pilate received a message on the balcony of his library. The message was a request from the legate of the tenth legion for increased imperial presence in Jerusalem for the upcoming Passover holiday.

Never a man to act in haste, the procurator sent a message back that he would be coming to the city himself to assess the situation. Pilate's presence, he opined to the legate, may somewhat assuage the situation.

When he reached Jerusalem later that month, Pilate found an array of executive duties awaiting him. Most involved internal squabbling among local authorities or military issues requiring arbitration. Pilate hated them all and, with the skill only an experienced administrator could have, he delegated most of them to lesser officials. The last and most laborious however could not be pawned off. Pilate had to confirm several death sentences handed down by the Sanhedrin. These criminals had a right to appeal to the Imperial government for leniency and most sought this avenue, though none were ever successful.

Reclining on his couch, a cup of Falernian in his hand, the procurator had his secretary read a list of the accused men and the crimes of which they had been convicted. When this was done, Pilate scheduled interviews with a chosen few and headed out toward the garden. On passing the secretary's table Pilate gazed lazily down at the parchments awaiting his signature.

"And just who is on the gibbet tomorrow?" inquired the procurator, a tinge of sarcasm in his voice.

The secretary reeled off four names without looking up. As he entered the garden, Pilate fancied he remembered one of the names and called back for the secretary to repeat them.

On hearing them a second time, Pilate's interest was piqued. He made a mental note to investigate further. With that, he sought relief from the heat of the day.

The prisoner Gestas was accused of the highest of crimes, sedition and treason against Tiberius himself. It was a capital crime, and Gestas was to pay with his life. Of the three condemned men in the cell with him, one had been convicted of a similar crime against Rome. The third an obscure wandering rabbi, had been accused of inciting a temple riot, and had been judged by the Sanhedrin, a sentence which Pilate had to confirm. The fourth inmate an insane career criminal from Ein-Geddi, had killed a centurion in a fit of rage.

The condemned cell was small mean affair. It also stank of feces. The twenty five cubit square cage had been built to house one; in this case it held four. The prisoners were forced to spend twenty four hours a day in the cell, so any excuse to get out, however briefly, was used.

The avenue to ensure a breath of fresh air before one's sentence was carried out was to appeal to Rome. This ensured the condemned man of an audience with the highest imperial official in Jerusalem, in this case Pilate.

The procurator disliked the dungeons. They smelt, and he had a keen sense of smell. Holding his breath Pilate descended the narrow stairway to the cells below. His escort, a large, ugly looking guard of Germanic descent, motioned him to follow down the dark passage way beneath the temple. Pilate coughed. The air was disgusting.

On approaching the condemned cell, Pilate stopped, waiting for an all clear signal from his escort, and peered in through the small window in the door. His eyes ran quickly over the wretched figures inside. He fixed his gaze on a man sat in cross legged position on the floor. Looking at the guard and nodding as if to confirm something, Pilate then turned and left. The guard, speaking in broken Aramaic, yelled through the insert.

"Gestas, to your feet."

Gestas rose slowly and shuffled in the direction of the door.

Pilate felt distinctly uncomfortable that morning; something was weighing terribly on his mind.

When the prisoner Gestas was led into the palace chamber, Pilate thought to motion the guards to leave, but instead addressed the prisoner in Greek. He spoke clearly and precisely.

"It has been a long time." said Pilate staring at the wretched prisoner in front of him.

Gestas, his beard matted and hair unkempt, showing all the contempt he could for the man sitting in front of him replied, "Not long enough." Then after some hesitation he added, "Father."

"I'm not your father," snapped Pilate glaring at his prisoner.

"So you say," said Gestas. "But my mother said otherwise." His chains rattled as he tried to move his arms.

"Your mother," said Pilate, raising the level of his voice slightly. "was a guardhouse whore."

Gestas looked long and hard at the procurator. "Why do you deny me?" he asked.

Pilate, the prisoner's stench and the infernal heat making him all the more miserable, motioned with his hand for the guards to remove Gestas. He poured himself some wine and began to think. The procurator thought for sometime, he felt trapped and needed a miracle.

Ordering his secretary to put down his thoughts on paper. Pilate sent a brief note outlining his problem to the Sanhedrin. In this dispatch Pilate asked that in exchange for condemning a radical Rabbi from Nazareth named Yeshua, a sentence which he had yet to confirm, the procurator and ultimate Tiberian authority requested the release of Gestas, a former employee of his in Caesarea.

Pilate was awoken early that fateful Nisan morning; the crowds that had streamed into Jerusalem for Passover had a riotous element. Pilate thought everyone from prophet to poisoner had some representation. Rising quickly, he washed and ran over his plan.

The message he had sent the Sanhedrin the previous evening had thus far gone unanswered and Pilate was becoming nervous. He strolled backward and forward across the palace floor deliberately avoiding the patterned parts of the tiling. After some time he noticed a figure enter the palace garden. He assumed it to be Caiaphas, the high priest.

The procurator was correct in his assumption; Caiaphas had personally come with a reply to Pilate's request. It was hot outside, and the two men sought the shade of a palm tree by the main fountain. After the usual niceties, the subject turned to the procurator's request.

Caiaphas indicated that he cared little who was spared that day so long as it was not the Rabbi from Nazareth, Yeshua.

Pilate said he was only too happy to oblige by confirming the death sentence of Yeshua of Nazareth. He then repeated the names of the three condemned men slowly to Caiaphas.

"Yeshua, Bar-abba and Dismas." said the procurator, "are to be executed this evening. Gestas is to be freed tonight and expelled from Judea. You shall receive the warrants by noon." He looked the high priest in the eye and repeated his statement.

Caiaphas nodded his assent, excused himself and left.

The procurator's eyes followed Caiaphas as he left the garden. Then his brow furrowed. He was worried. The Procurator did not trust the high priest.

Caiaphas, for his part did not trust the procurator. The lunatic from Nazareth needed executing, true, but the high priest had bigger fish to fry. He had been made aware of Pilate's interest in the prisoner Gestas some days prior. Caiaphas suspected a relationship between the two men, although he did not know what form it took. He surmised it was deep, if the procurator was to intervene in such mundane affairs.

Caiaphas needed to even the score with Pilate for the murder of some temple elders by Roman soldiers acting under imperial authority. Caiaphas knew that once the warrants were submitted no one would check the prisoners' identities, the high priest had a plan to settle his score with the procurator.

Reclining once again on his couch the procurator was thoughtful, once again wishing to take a stroll along the cliffs of Calabria. In his thoughts he drifted back to his youth before he taken up government service, the rolling waves and bright sandy coves.

His thoughts were interrupted by the head of the palace guard. It appeared the rabbi, Yeshua of Nazareth, had made a final appeal to Rome and Pilate was obliged to interview him. Pilate motioned to the head of the guard to bring the prisoner in.

Pilate was not in the mood for eastern philosophy that morning and he vowed to avoid engaging the man in idle conversation. Stretching his legs and yawning, he poured himself a cup of water and drank deeply.

"I've just finished with the last lunatic talking about fatherhood," said Pilate to his secretary, the irritation very evident in his voice.

"Now another idiot, this one talking about being the son of God," Rolling his eyes and motioning to the centurion, he added, "Let's do this."

The man brought before Pilate that morning was short and bedraggled and smelt of urine. The palace guard stood over him threateningly. Pilate considered him so insignificant that it was some moments before he gazed in the prisoner's direction.

"Alright. Did you incite others to destroy the temple?" asked Pilate.

The prisoner Yeshua simply smiled at Pilate dumbly.

"You," said Pilate starting again, doing his best to ignore Yeshua's smile which was making him a little uncomfortable, "claim to be the son of God."

Pilate poured himself some water, wishing it was wine.

"That's not quite right," started Yeshua. "I merely said..."

Pilate screwed his eyes as if in pain. "Shut up," he said.

"As you wish hegemon," answered Yeshua. The same serene smile was still on his face.

The procurator felt uneasy talking to this man. He did not appear scared or even worried about his impending fate.

"Crimes against Caesar are punishable by death," declared the Procurator." Your case however is somewhat marginal, you don't appear to have committed any imperial crime, the tetrarch has refused to confirm your sentence. Now I have to deal with you."

The procurator stood up and pulled his toga tight before saying.

"You appear to have inflamed some others of your ilk, and the Sanhedrin wants you punished. Take that grin off your face you miserable man. This is serious."

"There will come a time when there is no more crime, nor any need for punishment," began Yeshua, still smiling.

Pilate again stopped him short by holding up his hand, he needed this maniac to admit to a crime, and it was becoming difficult. The next few minutes were taken up by Pilate's secretary asking the prisoner various questions about his origins. Leaning against a column with his arms folded, Pilate stared out into the palace garden, Yeshua's answers barely audible to him. The Procurator's interest was however piqued when the Rabbi, after being asked the object of his teachings mentioned sacrificing oneself for the truth.

"You have been quoted as saying you would sacrifice yourself for the truth." stated Pilate.

"Or to save another." added the Rabbi.

"Shut up," snapped Pilate again.

The Procurator's mind was elsewhere, walking along the Calabria coast. Suddenly Pilate opened his eyes; a thought had started in his mind. Maybe he opined, this idiot did not need to have committed a crime. Pilate thought long and hard before starting. When he did it was with the articulation of an educated man.

"There is another who shares your beliefs in the dungeon with you; he is too scared to reveal himself. If you believe what you say, give your life for him." Pilate surprised even himself with his logic. The head of the palace guard smirked.

"Gladly," said the Rabbi smiling.

That was easy thought the procurator. Sometimes, he reasoned, power had its advantages. He was now free to negotiate Gestas' freedom. No one would remember this lunatic from Nazareth.

Pilate at last felt somewhat more comfortable if this maniac wanted to give his life to save others he was going to take full advantage. As the young man left his presence, shuffling between two centurions the Procurator walked over to a sink. Using a large ewer full of water he washed his hands. He then ordered his secretary sign the death warrants.

Joseph Caiaphas was a patient man. This attribute did not fail him that fateful afternoon. It was some hours before the procurator's secretary arrived with the confirmation of the sentences from the Imperial authority. Caiaphas took them and nodded in assent. He then walked quickly down the alleyway leading to the dungeons.

Arriving in front of the condemned cell, he named those to be executed to the escort and guard, adding that in honor of the great feast of Passover, the imperial authorities had chosen to spare Bar-abba. The pardoned man, looking relieved, and very surprised headed out of the prison the same way that the high priest had entered. Entering the alleyway he looked furtively around before disappearing into the crowd.

The condemned men were forced to carry their own methods of execution to Golgotha. It was a long walk from the palace dungeons to place of execution. Throngs of onlookers lined the streets to view the sad entourage as it made its way through Jerusalem's narrow streets. Some occasionally laughed and jeered but most looked on with only quaint interest.

Within two hours, the condemned men were on their respective gibbets. They had however several more hours suffering to endure before sunset. The soldiers and crowds generally lost interest at dark, when the centurions put them out of their misery.

When Pilate summoned Caiaphas to the Palace of Herod, again Pilate looked beaten. His shoulders slumped and his eyes sunken, he stood with his back to the doorway staring out at the city he despised. The high priest looked at the procurator, a victorious glint in his eye.

"A mistake I'm sure, hegemon." Caiaphas spoke carefully and deliberately not wishing to gloat on his vengeance, "The guards confused the men, a terrible mistake."

The procurator swung around, his gaze fixed like a snake on the high priest. The look was one of a man knowing that his power was greatest, the look of a man about to unleash that power.

"I believe," said Pilate slowly and deliberately, "that you have a son with application in Bethlehem?"

Caiaphas's cheeks reddened, he only hoped the messenger to flee had got to his son on time.

"Good day, High Priest." added Pilate.

Lastly, the procurator summoned Longinus, the head of the execution squad, to his chamber later that evening. Bidding him to sit and refresh himself, he inquired as to the afternoon's events.

"Did any of them have anything to say, Longinus?" inquired the Procurator, making a poor attempt at disinterest.

"Caiaphas's thaumatologist whined and moaned a little, I put him out of his misery." The centurion attempted unsuccessfully to sound humane as he drank his wine. Bidding Longinus to continue until he hated eaten his fill, Pilate started out toward the garden stepping deliberately on the stone slabs which made a path through the shrubbery.

"Oh, pardon me, Hegemon," the centurion started again, calling after him. "The criminal on the right gibbet kept on saying something about his father."

"What did he say?" snapped Pilate.

"Why have you forsaken me?" replied Longinus shrugging his shoulders.

The procurator winced and fixed his gaze on the horizon. It was dark, and in the clouds he imagined he could see Rome. Suddenly the heavens opened and it began to rain.

The Stranger on the Shore

Beaches and memories are inextricably linked. Often our deepest thoughts and passions come back to us as we amble up sand dunes, watching gentle waves rolling in with the tide.

Harriet Woodcraft had come to live at this beach, which she presumed would be her last, with her husband of thirty years Samuel. It was a second marriage for both of them, and a happy one. Both had no regrets and happily coexisted in a cottage hidden in the dunes where the Delaware Bay meets the Atlantic Ocean.

Harriet's memories were very much her own and because they often predated Samuel she was reluctant to share them with anyone. So afternoon walks along the bay picking up pebbles were a therapy for her and she was comfortable with it this way.

One July, however, a couple of events occurred that stirred her memory palace. Her daughter Kate came to stay, bringing Harriet's grandchildren. It was quite a treat for Harriet and bonding with the children was particularly fun. There were endless walks down the dunes as she got to know her descendants.

Other feelings were however stirred. Kate was the product of a previous marriage and her presence sent Harriet thinking back to a time before Samuel. Her memories washed around her brain like the rising tide, her thoughts and feelings plummeting to the darkest ocean depths. The afternoon walks became contemplative and Harriet spent longer than usual picking up pebbles as she threaded up the shoreline.

Immediately prior to her first marriage Harriet had been involved briefly with a young Englishman. The spires of Oxford had been the backdrop to the affair which had been torrid and hasty. Her first husband, to whom she was engaged at the time, had gone on an academic tour of Eastern Europe and left her alone in England. Dick, her lover was a bright, learned Cornishman up at Balliol College reading Classics. He had a certain intellectual charm. The sort who sparks a women's interest with the dour intelligence oft found in academics.

Harriet had fallen wildly in love and the affair which ensued was tragic for both of them. She longed to take this diffident scholar along the New Jersey beaches of her youth and roll in the incoming tide. To share with him the shells she had collected as a child and the secrets she had buried in the sand. Harriet loved Dick as much as her own zest for life and he loved her, although his personality precluded his being as emotional.

They had met in parks and college libraries and Harriet had been introduced to a world which she had not known existed. He in turn had benefitted greatly from her bubbly personality and became, during the few months of the affair, far more sociable.

Harriet was engaged. Not that it was a problem to break it, but her fiancé liked beaches. He liked sitting and walking on them, the feel of sand between his toes. Dick was not a beach guy, if there is such a thing in England. He liked formality and structure. Harriet doubted he had ever been to a real beach. Most of the beaches she had been to in England were pebbled, rocky and cold with incessant cawing of gulls.

So the affair was ended almost as soon as it began and Harriet left with her memories which she stored away in a very special place. She married her fiancé Charles, but regretted it and they divorced after fifteen years and two children. Harriet had half hoped that in divorcing Charles the memories of Dick, so long locked away would dissipate, but they did not. She found herself mentioning his name more than once in private...

Harriet's beach was a flat sandy one, stretching for miles along the Delaware Bay shoreline. It was quiet, even in the height of summer Harriet had few companions to share her memories with. The sand hills which backed the beach were broken every fifty yards or so by private residences, most of which were owner occupied. It was a neat little community, a great place to fade out along with your memories, to watch sunsets in the sunset of your life.

One particular afternoon found Harriet on her walk, picking up brightly colored pebbles and strangely shaped shells when she noticed ahead of her a couple sat on deckchairs at the ebbing tide line.

The brightly colored umbrella marked them as not regular beach people. Harriet closed in on the chairs slowly, lost in her afternoon dreams. As she got closer she smiled and the couple returned the compliment. Harriet noticed how pale they were. Not much sun in their lives she thought.

"Good afternoon," she said smiling.

Harriet had an infectious smile, the recipients felt as if they were the centre of attention.

The man tipped a large sun hat.

"You too," he said.

A sunhat, fancy, thought Harriet, and an umbrella. These were definitely snowbirds. Harriet continued down the beach wrapped in her thoughts, stopping every now and then to admire the flat Delaware Bay which sat shimmering in the sun. She turned back toward her house at the next moraine; her return speed was always quicker.

She passed the two deckchairs again, but now only the man remained, his companion was nowhere to be seen. This time Harriet slowed down her approach, she had not had company all day and the empty deckchair seemed inviting. She gave the stranger a big grin and said, "The bay is calm today."

"Are you a local?" inquired the man, his accent distinctly English.

"Yes, I suppose I am," replied Harriet. "I've lived here these last thirty years. I can tell you're not."

The man smiled. Harriet had inkling that he seemed vaguely familiar. His nuances, she was sure she had seen them somewhere before.

"No I'm just passing through," said the stranger, "I am looking for some one."

"Someone special?" asked Harriet. This was getting very exciting she thought.

"Yes. I have a message for her," said the stranger.

Just then a women's voice, which seemed very distant to Harriet called from above the dunes. Harriet did not catch what she said, but the stranger stood up immediately, tipped his hat and headed in the direction of the house behind them.

Remembering someone who you knew for a few months half a century ago is difficult and Harriet was not quite sure. Beaches, though, are magical places and Harriet's mind drew the stranger forty five years younger, the same Celtic features and tall frame. Was it Dick? Or was her mind and the beach playing tricks with her? Her recollection of him as a young man was quite clear, in fact for all these years she imagined him as her silent partner on her walks. The conversations she had held had been with him. Private and special and now out of the blue....it surely could not be.

The following day Harriet resolved to take a morning and afternoon stroll in hope of catching sight of the stranger. A northeast gale was blowing in the Atlantic, and the surf in the bay was rough. Wave after wave of white caps rolled in giving the bay a tempestuous look. Harriet wrapped in her thoughts mused that the beach itself had recalled those days in Oxford.

There is something about the safety of a bay in rough weather. Life continues as before, try as they might the waves will never push their way up the shoreline.

Thoughts too were pushing into Harriet's deepest places. Probing rollers washed her most sacred feelings out into the open. She had spent a lifetime secreting these emotions and did not want to give them up, but back came the memories of nights of passion in his rooms at Oxford, staying up all night telling him her childhood secrets and devoted to his every move. He was the attentive companion, fascinating her with his brilliance, wit and perception. Ah, if only life had been so easy.

The strangers were no where in sight that day. The wind had blown them off the bay and Harriet, although a little disappointed was also a little thankful. Her secrets and passions were safe for another day.

Storms move quickly through the Atlantic that time of year and the following day the beach front was its usual calm and sedate self. Harriet ever thoughtful picked her way along the beach through the mess of shells and horseshoe crabs. Her mind wandering, her emotions placid like the bay waters.

The strangers were out on the bay. Their multi-colored umbrella was a monstrosity. Harriet felt somewhat apprehensive at the sight of it, she thought to turn back and, for the first time in years, end her walk early. Harriet did not like the feelings that the stranger stirred in her, it was as if he possessed the key to her emotions.

Eventually Harriet decided to walk briskly past the strangers as if they had never met, but as she got closer her idea of passing behind the deck chairs was dashed when the stranger looked her way.

She could see that the man had no companion today. He was sat alone on his deck chair looking at the horizon. As Harriet approached he adjusted his sun glasses and smiled.

"Hello again," said the stranger. Harriet studied his features more closely now.

"Hi," said Harriet, "are you staying long?"

If this was Dick he did not recognize her.

"No I leave tomorrow afternoon," he replied.

"Did you deliver your message?" asked Harriet.

"Sadly no," said the stranger, "we could not find the person we sought."

"Where is your wife?" Harriet was vaguely aware of the leading manner of her question.

"She is my sister," he replied, his sunglasses staring directly at Harriet.

"I was here to look for my grandson, amongst other things," he continued. "His mother brought him to America fifteen years ago. I have not seen him since."

"I'm sorry." said Harriet momentarily wondering what a lengthy separation from her own grandchildren would feel like. "My own grandchildren were here a week or so ago."

There was an uncomfortable silence and Harriet did not know how to break it.

"There is nothing greater than grandchildren," the stranger commented. "I have many, but my life seems incomplete without this one." His voice was low and melancholy. Harriet listened intently for any sound or pronunciation that would indicate this was her long lost lover.

The stranger, however, did not appear in the mood for conversation and after exchanging a few niceties Harriet continued up the bay on her walk. When she returned the deck chair was empty.

A morning walk was what Harriet took the following day, as early as she could get away. Her steps up the beach were fast, she did not dawdle. Almost to her relief she spotted a lone deckchair on the sand.

This is it she thought. I must speak my mind and ask this stranger if he is the man I have loved most of my life. This would be such a relief she thought. Approaching the deckchair she held her breath before exchanging a pleasantry.

"Good morning. I thought you were leaving?" she said standing directly between the stranger and the sea.

"I'm just taking one last look." replied the stranger.

"May I ask your name?" said Harriet only vaguely aware her left foot was digging a hole in the sand.

"Sure", said the stranger. "My name is Robert."

If she was disappointed Harriet did not show it visibly, but inside her stomach churned. She felt sick, stupid and relieved all at once. So this was not her long lost lover.

"Are you English?" Harriet asked vacantly...

"Yes indeed." replied the stranger. "The accent always gives it away."

"I was at school in Oxford." offered Harriet...

"Really, when?" inquired the stranger pulling himself up in his deckchair, his attention piqued.

"In the late sixties," answered Harriet, the wind catching her hair and blowing it across her tanned face.

"Then we were contemporaries," said the stranger. "I was at Balliol."

Harriet was quiet for a while before she spoke.

"I was at Hartford, I had a good friend at Balliol, and his name was Richard Sowerby. People called him Dick."

Harriet thought it odd to be talking of him the past tense. She felt the name, unspoken in forty five years echo up the beach as if released from a shell. The wind, the beach, the water all spoke his name.

"Yes, I knew him, brilliant fellow. Shame he died so young." said the stranger, his last words seeming to trail off.

The beach stopped breathing. Harriet did not know for how long she held her breath, it felt as if she had been holding it all these years.

"When did he die?" she asked quietly.

"He drowned in 75 or 76 as I recall," said the stranger. "His wife was inconsolable."

The ebbing waves sucked Harriet's emotions away, slowly lifting the veil of secrecy which had protected them for years. She was scared. What would be revealed? Were all her memories inextricably linked? Now this one was destroyed. Would they all tumble like dominoes? Harriet was so deeply lost in thought she forgot the stranger sat in front of her.

"Are you okay?" the stranger asked.

Harriet did not answer immediately, she waited for her emotions to settle, for her other memories to retake their new places in her mind's ocean. When the waves in her mind had broken and scuttled up the beach, she smiled.

"I'm fine," she said. "I just had a bad dream I suppose."

"Well," said the stranger. "Time and tide wait for no man, so I must be on my way."

"I'm sorry you didn't find what you were looking for," said Harriet wholeheartedly.

The stranger stood up and held out his hand to Harriet saying. "Who says I didn't find what I was looking for?" and standing up he added, "Goodbye Harriet."

He folded up his deckchair and was halfway back up the beach before Harriet realized that she had never told him her name. She started after him and thought of even yelling but stopped herself. One surprise was enough for one day.

Later that evening Harriet, although sad, was also happy. Her husband of thirty years was at her side watching the sunset. Her memories had not cheated on him. Dick had died before she had even known Samuel. Her memories and her beach walks were safe forever. Not knowing how to proceed, she stared down at the shells in her hands. They were clean and bright, the inhabitants long gone. On the bay the tide began to turn.

The Emperor's New Clothes

The morning Ian Ritter went completely insane was a morning otherwise unmemorable. The hazy morning sun typical of late July, strong enough to burn skin yet weak enough to forget hats. Ian Ritter had seen hundreds of mornings like these, yet this particular one catalyzed something in his troubled mind.

Ian Ritter was a man of habit. He rose early and his first activity was to shower. Obsessively cleaning imaginary dirt from behind his ears he hummed softly to himself. The tune was regal, and that was fitting because Ian had gone to bed the previous night a house husband, and he had woken up an Emperor.

Proud and surprised by his newfound position Ian decided to behave accordingly. His children need not be awakened for school, because, as the sons of royalty, education was a formality. Ian smiled to himself as he imagined honorary doctorates of letters being bestowed upon his sons.

His wife, a lawyer, had already left for work. Rather than clean up behind her as he usually did, Ian spoke to an imaginary maid, ordering her to clean up the mess. After taking a leisurely breakfast of eggs and coffee, which in the absence of kitchen staff he was forced to make himself he planned his day.

There would be engagements to keep, for when one is an emperor, the common folk must be appeased and entertained. Now, thought Ian, "Who was it who requested an audience today?" ...he thought deeply, his head in his hands, and finally remembered it was a minor bank official from the local town. He could not imagine what the man wanted with him, he would like to blow him off, but as a favor to his empress he had granted him an audience. He hoped the interview would not be long; these sorts of people were very tedious and tended to get on his nerves.

The doorbell rang distantly; Ian jumped up at the sound and with a new spring in his step walked to the door. He opened the front door with gusto fitting of a monarch, whilst bemoaning the lack of good house staff.

On the doorstep stood the postman. Smartly dressed in blue and clean shaven, he spoke tersely to Ian. Ian did not care for his tone.

"I've been ringing this bell for twenty minutes," he snapped. "Are you Ian Ritter?"

"Mind your mouth, Postie," replied Ian. "I'll have some respect out of you when you're addressing your superiors."

The postman was a little taken aback by Ian's rhetoric. He repeated his question. "Are you Ian Ritter?"

Ian mused that to continue conversation with this oaf was useless. He obviously had little respect for majesty, and Ian promptly slammed the door in the astonished postman's face. Returning to his eggs and coffee, he decided that his kingdom really needed some discipline, and he thought that maybe the introduction of martial law would be an idea. Giving it deeper thought, he decided that a little capital punishment would be useful and wondered why he ever suspended it. Rummaging around on the table he found a pen and paper and neatly he wrote "executions" and underlined it.

Ian Ritter did not consider himself a brutal monarch, and it was only after some time and soul searching that he scrawled the name postie under his heading.

"Argh, the anguish," he thought to himself, the anguish of power. He really wanted to spare Postie, but laws are laws.

For the next ten minutes, Ian Ritter contemplated his day and then, realizing the governess had not woken his children yet, he strolled across to their rooms. Both were locked, and he knocked on the doors for several minutes, still there was no reply.

He may have knocked all day had not a lone fly buzzed up the hallway. It was a large bluebottle and Ian could make out its eyes. When you are as omnipotent as Ian Ritter you heed man and beast alike. Ian Ritter thought the fly was telling him something.

"Come with me," said the fly.

"Where?" asked Ian.

"Why to the palace, your Majesty." said the fly. "Your people need you." said the fly.

"I cannot my good fly," answered Ian Ritter. "I have an audience with a minor official on the state of the kingdom's banking sector." He then added, "And I have to execute the postman."

The fly was joined by a whole multitude of flies. They buzzed around Ian Ritter's head.

"See, Your Majesty," said the fly, "your people need you. Besides the Postman has not finished his rounds yet."

Ian Ritter had to agree. If the people needed him he must go, for it is the burden of a monarch to put his subjects first. He wished his confounded children would wake up. It would be useful for them to see how a kingdom should be run, but he must make haste.

It was then that Ian Ritter contrived a cunning plan. Rather than appear in all his majesty, Ian decided to surprise his subjects by going in disguise. So he quickly took off his dressing gown and replaced it with a beach towel. He thought this should fool them and give him some opportunity to see how his kingdom was working without being too intrusive. Quickly grabbing his crown from the table, Ian left his house with his flies following behind him.

The lack of a carriage puzzled Ian. Then he surmised he must have given his staff the day off. Above him, the flies were becoming impatient and Ian did not want to keep his subjects waiting. The swarm followed the lead bluebottle down the street. Ian Ritter jumped into his car and followed them.

The county courthouse was an imposing affair. Built in late Victorian style it exuded elegance and justice, a place quite fitting for an emperor to address his subjects. It was composed of two modest-sized buildings which were served by a parking lot.

Ian Ritter arrived in his car. He had sped most of the way; the infernal flies would not slow down. His subjects were waiting, they claimed, no need to stop; the road is yours, Majesty. He pulled his car into the courthouse lot, parked in the space allotted for royalty and preceded into the building crown in hand.

Small towns have little security, and Ian Ritter merrily strolled the halls for several minutes before being accosted by a security guard. The guard, a tall lank fellow in his thirties seemed surprised to see him. Ian had somewhat expected this, it was an impromptu visit and the man did not know he was in disguise. To alert the slow-witted fellow Ian put on his crown.

The insolent security guard gave Ian the same stare as the postman had, and for a moment Ian fancied they may be the same man.

"Afternoon my good fellow," said Ian staring imperiously down his nose.

The security guard was still staring at Ian. It was some moments before he spoke.

"Is everything okay, Sir?" he asked.

It suddenly dawned upon Ian Ritter that the man did not recognize him in his disguise, even with the crown on.

"It's okay my good fellow," said Ian." I came here in disguise so as not to alarm anyone."

The security guard did not reply. He walked over to a nearby desk and picked up the phone. Not wishing to alarm Ian, he bade him sit down and for safety's sake added "Your Majesty".

Ian Ritter did not wish to sit and firmly told the insolent oaf that he was wanted in courtroom number one. When the guard got up to stop him, Ian Ritter slapped him across the face and reminded him that he too could face execution should the need arise.

Just then he caught sight of the flies hovering impatiently in front of the door to courtroom number one. Ian pushed open the swinging doors, ignoring the usher. The security guard, getting over the shock of being slapped, followed him.

The court was in session when Ian Ritter walked calmly over to the defense table where his wife sat. Sitting casually, one foot on the floor he addressed the defense counsel.

"empress." he said clearing his throat."I wish to address my people."

His wife looked at Ian in disbelief."What are you doing?" .she asked

"I," started Ian Ritter. "your monarch, am making a surprise appearance and speech today."

"Ian," said his wife, "What's wrong?"

"Why nothing." said Ian Ritter, staring at her with amusement. His wife did not seem happy. Ian was perplexed until the fly reminded him he was in disguise. Of course he thought the disguise was so good that even his wife did not recognize him. Oh well thought Ian, I had better reveal myself to these simple peasants.

Standing on the defense attorney's desk, Ian Ritter made an impassioned appeal to his people, most of whom had disappeared. Gesticulating wildly and at times running out of breath, Ian explained the current lack of discipline within his kingdom and the need to return to martial law. Adjusting his crown, he asked the fly now buzzing some two feet above his eye level why his people were not listening.

"We are your people," replied the fly, with a touch of sarcasm that Ian fancied.

"Mind your tongue insect," commanded Ian Ritter.

"As your majesty pleases," answered the fly.

"Now where has my wife gone?" thought Ian Ritter. "Typical of women, always sneaking off. That's why men are rulers. Women are weak. Ahh, thought Ian, the rest of the flies have found me. He heard them buzzing around his head..... God, he thought, the buzzing was annoying.

The flies buzzing in Ian Ritter's ear got louder and louder until it became unbearable and he had to sit down. Eventually feeling the pressure of the moment, he lay down and decided to take a little rest before continuing his speech.

Ian Ritter's nearly naked body lay slumped over the defense counsel's table, his eyes fixed on the ceiling fan. He was dead, shot through the head.

What Will George Do Next?

As the mayor of Hope these last two years, life had been easy for George. Daily affairs had been chugging along effortlessly. This suited George because he really had no head for politics and disliked the inner workings of government, preferring to spend most of his time watching the town's baseball team or walking his pet dog, Goliath.

The country of Hope was large, occupying the whole of a peninsula, bordered only on the north by the impoverished country of Need, from which it was separated only by a long meandering river named Betterment.

Hope was subsistent mainly on trade. It had been founded some two hundred years before by a handful of missionaries, who, landing by mistake on its luscious shores, had lost all interest in returning to their land of origin, Oppression.

Once ensconced in Hope, the missionaries bearing bible and gun had tried to convert the handful of native peoples. When this had failed, they had, with the blessing of the Monarch back in Oppression, decided on forceful removal.

Turkeys were prevalent in Hope and the missionaries invited their co-inhabitants to a harvest feast during which, to ensure their guests comfort, they had provided blankets infected with smallpox. The natives, with no immunity to prevent the virulent spread of the disease had all but died out during the winter. This left the missionaries free to occupy the territory and farm it to feed the ever-increasing flow of immigrants from Oppression.

The last two hundred years had not passed uneventfully, however. Hope had been forced to fight a costly war with its mother state, Oppression. Although no one was really sure of the reasoning, Hope had prevailed and Oppression sat down like a wounded cat, licking its paws, watching eagerly for the fledgling republic to fail.

But fail it had not, and through a mixture of ingenuity, travail and open immigration it turned itself very rapidly into a model for other countries.

One of the first problems the young country had been forced to deal with was a labor shortage. Hope had been forced to import a good deal of slave labor from a less-developed continent to the west and this had resulted in an ever-multiplying number of slaves, all of whom wanted a say in their new country's affairs.

The missionaries, now long dead, had not foreseen such an issue, but in the ever changing environment Hope's government was forced to address the issue. This they did with great pragmatism, promising better conditions and emancipation for all Hope's residents. A series of internal struggles had followed, though the country of Hope took all these within her stride. Thus by the time we get to George's tenure things were chugging along quite nicely on the surface. Beneath it however old resentments simmered.

One of Hope's greatest achievements was the transmission of information by television. The ever-paranoid elders discovered that by giving their residents a steady diet of mindless drama, game shows and religion they could somewhat control their thoughts and actions. Thus, twenty years before this story, Hope's council had passed a law requiring that all households were required to have a least one television set in each room.

Economically, Hope dominated the area. Its residents' endless desire for consumer products made it the single largest buying block in the hemisphere. This and skillful market manipulation by some of the more financially savvy members of the government had turned the once sleepy peninsula of Hope into a large vital economy with several bustling metropolises.

Thus by our story's start, Hope, originally founded as a beacon for those seeking sanctuary from Oppression, had somewhat lost it's way. George the newly elected mayor had vowed to reinstate traditional values and bring Hope in line with the philosophy of its founding fathers.

George, the mayor of Hope, had not always been a religious man. Much of his youth was spent in the general debauchery that prevailed in the country. George had indulged in the local grain alcohol and local women to such an extent that his parents had been forced to spend the majority of their spare time disguising or hiding their son's immoral behavior.

George's one true passion was baseball. He spent hours on the local grounds trying out for professional teams. His height and lack of physical prowess had caused rejection and disappointment, though. By the time he was thirty, George was an embittered alcoholic with no employment prospects.

Around this time, however, two events were to change the course of George's history. Firstly, his father, Big George was elected to the position of mayor by a mixture of cronyism and bribery; this gave George some hope of employment in his father's administration. The second was George's chance meeting with the Reverend Faith.

The Reverend Faith had come into George's life ten years ago. This towering figure of Protestant venom had spoken at George's alcohol rehabilitation meetings. George was impressed by the man's convictions and, looking for an early way to side step the court ordered dry out, embraced the redemption offered by Faith and hoped to harness its convictions to his own advantage.

Faith himself had also seen an avenue to further his personal goals and ever expanding religion, but did not entirely trust George, viewing him as a little shallow at times. So in order to cement their strange union, Faith insisted that George be force fed bottles of a sickly mixture he called 'Faith restorer'. So disgusting and objectionable was the concoction to George that he lived in continual fear of both Faith and his cure.

Thus George kept on his desk two bottles. The first, filled with grain alcohol was marked 'Temptation'. The second marked 'Faith', contained sickly syrup, disgusting to the palate. If George should ever find himself giving in to temptation, he simply reached for the second bottle and drank a nasty swig of Faith.

When Big George was unseated at the next election by Slick Willie, the Reverend Faith saw his opportunity. Carefully planning years ahead, he bought considerable news time to promote George's son for candidacy. Faith had already taken hold of much of the country mentally and, with what he figured would a little leg work within the urban areas, Faith could already smell victory.

With George's candidacy secured, Faith tried a short, sharp, shock treatment from his pulpits, painting George as a saint and savior of traditional values for Hope, now, he said, a country heading irrevocably in the direction of Need, its impoverished northern neighbor.

George, the most unlikely and unqualified candidate for high office in the history of Hope, ran against a lack-luster character named Shallow. Shallow, better educated and experienced for the job, inconceivably thought that by belittling George, he would highlight George's inadequacies. The reverse took effect. The general public sympathized with George's pathetic mispronunciations and lack of depth. The result was a tie that was broken by a coin toss on the baseball diamond at Pleasure. Faith himself officiated at the tossing and secreted a double-headed coin to ensure George's victory.

Thus George, semi-literate, inexperienced and with a far greater affinity for goats than his fellow man, became the mayor of Hope.

George's father Big George owned a world-class residence on the southern tip of Hope. Built on a promontory overlooking the vast southern ocean it afforded the elder George a sense of tranquility and removal from the problems of the outside world.

George and his father loved to race gas-guzzling speed boat up and down the long stretch of water, where in the company of invited guests they discussed matters relating to the perennial problem of Black Gold.

Black Gold was the life blood of Hope. Necessary for all but the most menial operations, the country drank it like thirsty dogs drink water.

So much in demand was it that Hope's leading economists had warned Big George during his tenure that the reserves were falling to a critical level and Hope should really find an alternative source of energy or else a larger supply base. Big George did not care for new fangled ways and instead sent his economists on a world tour to find new sources and deposits of Black Gold.

They returned empty-handed but noted in their reports to the Mayor that considerable deposits of Black Gold were indicated beneath the country of Greed, a one-party dictatorship in the west.

Hoping to persuade Greed to sell all its vast reserves to Hope, Big George indulged its tin pan Dictator Ras in a flattering display of cheap arms sales, which Greed in turn used mercilessly against its neighbor Want.

Both Greed and Want fought to a stalemate and, thirsty for investment, Greed was forced to lower the price of Black Gold to be more in line with Big George's price point.

With Want contained and Greed on its knees, Big George saw Hope's future as bright. His endless summer was marred, however, when a spoiler candidate entered the mayoral race and allowed Big George's opponent, Slick Willie, a sexually motivated misogynist, to prevail in that years election.

General Complacency, the newly appointed interior secretary believed passionately in isolationism. His motto, "It ain't our problem," had held well. Hope's citizens went about their daily business oblivious to world events. Complacency made sure that negative news reporting was kept to a minimum and the populace was encouraged to attend more baseball games and eat more beef burgers.

This suited George who had inadvertently purchased a large head of diseased cattle from his deputy Dick. The cattle made perfect beef burger meat and George made a handsome if unforeseen profit.

The attack that no one foresaw came in the fall. A group of militants from an obscure desert covered country named Repression, hijacked two planes and crashed landed them into George's new baseball field during a championship game, killing all the players and half the crowd.

George, who was in a classroom full of six-year-old children reading a story about a goat, at first dismissed the news as pandering to sensation by the opposition. Plus he was enjoying the goat story.

Upon being persuaded that Hope was under attack, George mobilized the under-trained and under-paid armed forces of the country and sought his revenge.

The commanders of George's army were Generals Shock and Awe, both failed farmers from Hope's interior. Neither had any practical knowledge or experience but had come recommended by Reverend Faith.

Shock and Awe were childhood friends of George's and the three had played countless games of risk as children. George had been told that their constant defeats of him on the board game were due to superior military tactics and not intellect.

Meeting Shock and Awe that day, George inveighed to them the importance of revenge and redemption. Standing up in his newly made cowboy boots designed with a four inch hidden heel, he found himself staring into the eyes of his two commanders.

"We'll smoke 'em and hang 'em," said the eager George.

"Well, George, wouldn't it be wiser to smoke 'em out, gut 'em and hang 'em?" asked Shock. "I'd like to gut 'em,"

George remembered as a child Shock gutting a pet goldfish while alive and then roasting the unfortunate fish on a spit.

"How do ya gut 'em?" asked George.

"With a knife," replied the bewildered Shock.

"Isn't that expensive?" asked George. "I mean that's a lot of knives."

"Yeah," answered Shock his square jaw moving like a ruminating bull. "But let's borrow the money from the Department of Education. I mean it's somewhat educational, learning how to gut. It's part of cookin' and farmin'."

George did not need anymore convincing. Clapping his friends on the back, he issued an immediate executive order allowing gutting as a reasonable way to obtain information.

Although, in our George's defense, he did not expect his new policy to be implemented at home, the Reverend Faith seized upon the opportunity.

He declared from his golden pulpit in Center City that gutting was a reasonable form of soul searching and would be sanctioned by Faith himself. Ever the pragmatist, George titled his new program 'Soul Searching.'

Meanwhile, far away across the ocean, the king of Repression was scratching his chin. It was a long chin totally covered by a beard, giving him the appearance of a water sodden mop.

Repression was a state which had come into being several decades earlier. The king, who had been living out his life as an obscure goatherd had against his will been installed by the departing colonial power, Oppression.

With little head for government, the king had spent the first years learning how to read. With this completed, he implemented many of the practices of the former rulers in the area of torture and bribery, allowing a slightly greater leeway to his torturers when dealing with females.

Ten years after coming to power, a shepherd boy not dissimilar to the king in origin, found a pile of dead sheep clustered around a water hole in the north of the kingdom. The sheep had inadvertently discovered Black Gold and the kingdom's fortunes were made.

Seizing on the opportunity, the half-literate monarch and his court proceeded to engage in trade with the land of Hope, the only country with surplus money and an appetite for Black Gold, similar to that of a hungry shark. The exchange of money and technology was massive and within a decade the king had suppressed all opposition to his rule and ensconced himself in a jeweled palace which could only be entered by his closest advisors.

As luck would have it both the king and the mayor of Hope (at the time Big George) had an affinity for goats and it was this common affinity which sealed a lifelong friendship between them. From then hence a steady stream of Black Gold left Repression in exchange for money and any other modern conveniences the King cared for.

Back in the land of Hope, George had a problem. His closest advisors were telling him that the miscreants who had destroyed the baseball game had come from the Kingdom of Repression.

"We need a diversion, sir," said his secretary that day.

It took some thinking before George and the deputy mayor, Dick, came up with a solution.

To the north of Repression lay the smaller country named Greed. This country, run by a psychotic dictator named Ras had incurred the wrath of Hope some years previously by attempting to increase the price of Black Gold and goats.

Hope's former colonial overseer Oppression, had long since abandoned its monarchy in favor of civil government. This government was headed by Tom Foolery, a recently elected glad mouther whose one claim to fame was that he had won a tiddly wink competition in high school. He also had a fondness for goats.

Thus the triumvirate was formed by the three goat loving heads of state: Hope, Oppression and Repression. This rather unholy alliance declared Greed a rogue state and called for the immediate overthrow of Ras.

That was all George needed. Summoning Shock and Awe again the gleeful mayor told them to immediately start bombing and invading Greed.

"Let us meet Greed with the full forces of Hope and Faith," the headlines read.

Then contacting the minister of information, George arranged to have several television shows broadcast nightly showing the citizens of Greed strangling puppies, pissing in fonts and performing other nefarious deeds.

Generals' Shock and Awe were not exactly sure how their much-lauded bombing campaign would fare. To be safe, they ordered heavier more destructive bombs so as not to waste any Black Gold on double flights.

His duties safely delegated to others, George went about his daily toil with his usual ambivalence. The one notable event during this time was that George, whose command of English was poor, had inadvertently coined a term for all non-citizens. The term was 'Hopeless' and fast became popular amongst his office staff so that within weeks everyone who was not born in the country of Hope was officially termed "Hopeless."

George was proud of himself until his brother pointed out that his own wife had originated from Need to the north of Hope. George avoided her awkward stare and later that week, as if to re-emphasize his commitment, commissioned the building of a large electric fence the length of Hope's northern border to stop the Hopeless in Need from entering Hope illegally. When it failed, Dick, George's deputy mayor, authorized a current of ten thousand volts to be run through it.

Our George, however, lost the stomach for his convictions when a goat farmer from the north was shown on television with a dead goat, fried black. George ordered instead a high frequency resonator, audible to animals installed at the border as a warning device; he did not want any more dead goats on his conscience. He would widen and deepen river Betterment.

The effect of George's bombing campaign, now called Shock and Awe by the jovial mayor, was devastating. Within three days, more by luck than judgment, the land of Greed had been partially reduced to rubble, without water, hospitals or electricity.

Once given the green light, Hope's ground forces, commanded by General Disarray, marched relatively unimpeded toward the capital of Greed. Securing all major airfields and power plants they established an almost air-tight security zone known as Peace in the city center, leaving it only to go on heavily armored details to quell uprising amongst the various ethnic groups which made up Greed.

George appeared nightly on television, telling tales of how the Hopeless were on the run and victory against Greed was within sight. Shock and Awe, in deference to their Mayor's foibles, allowed the motor-challenged George to fly a large fortress bomber over the shores of Hope in a spectacular display of audacity.

The former dictator of Greed was captured and publicly displayed on television, then beheaded in public in accordance with local tradition. The executioner Haq was himself elected President for life the following day by coin toss.

All the blood and strife in the region had come to the attention of Greed's main neighbor Want; Want was an oligarchy run by a few fanatical clerics and rabble rousers who saw their chance to grabs Greed's huge reserves of Black Gold for themselves. Want knew that to directly take on Hope was useless. Want needed a more cunning plan.

Wants' nominal head of government, Submission, was thrice tried for forgery under the preceding rulers, but had, on account of his vocal opposition to Hope, found favor with the incoming theocrats.

The plan which Submission implemented was a simple one. Every home in Greed was to receive a copy of Submission's autobiography entitled 'Dealing with Oppression', complete with photographs of the president personally beheading or torturing political opponents.

The result was to drive fear into the hearts of Greed's citizens who now faced the harsh choice between bombs and racks.

By year's end, the interim government reigned in Greed, propped up by the omnipresent General Disarray. Generals Shock and Awe saw to it that little of this was publicized in Hope. Thus Hope's citizens went about their daily business uninformed and uncaring. The baseball stadium had been rebuilt, and everyone had somewhat forgotten the terrible events of the previous year.

The following year George was visited briefly one afternoon by his secretary of finance, Dr. Creditcrisis.

The minister requested the meeting to point out to George that Hope was spending an inordinate amount of money on its war with Greed.

"We may have to cut back a little," he told George, pen in hand.

"Okay," said George, uninterested. "Do what you have to do."

Dr. Creditcrisis started by devaluing Hope's currency. This had little effect. The citizens of Hope were used to spending and were not about to stop.

The minister handled this issue skillfully, giving each citizen a right to borrow money on plastic cards. The unsuspecting citizens spent the non-existent money with the same vigor as if it were real. Within six months the average citizen had borrowed the value of his life's earnings. Not that it bothered him; money had ceased to mean anything to him anyway.

Secretary Reason had not had a fun time of it in George's administration, always over-looked, never listened to. He spent most of his time idly waiting at George's door seeking an audience. George had little time for Reason, believing him a tricky fellow given to twisting facts to his own advantage.

In recent months however, Reason had become increasingly popular, people preferring his dour intellectual approach to that of Shock and Awe.

Seizing the moment, Reason barged his way through the crowd of people outside George's door and stood there stoically, refusing to move until he was heard. Reluctantly, George agreed to a meeting, but placed the stipulation that Reason should not ask any awkward questions that may hold any double meanings.

Secretary Reason was a pragmatic man. Knowing philosophical arguments would be lost on George, he tried a simpler more understandable approach.

"Sir, we are spending all our money on knives for soul searching and bombs for Shock and Awe. We will soon be broke. You know what that means: no more baseball."

George, who had been expecting this question, was quick with his response.

"Secretary Creditcrisis has informed me that we have enough money for baseball."

Reason scratched his long earlobe. This was going to be tough. In his mind, he pulled up an image of George from many years prior.

"What about the goats?" he asked cautiously.

"What about them?" asked George.

"Well, the Reverend Faith has stated that the soul searching policies he implemented at your behest also apply to Greed's goats."

"What," yelled George, "those furry little ones as well?"

"Yes," replied Reason. "They're all to be gutted."

George slumped in his chair. His boots were hurting him and he was thinking about a pet goat he had fed as a child.

"Added to that, General Disarray has declared all the goats in Greed outlaws. He wants them hunted down to extermination."

Dismissing the thought of dead goats from his head, George yelled at Reason to get out and stop invading his space. Reason dually obliged and only hoped he had sown enough of a seed in the Mayor's head to start a thought process.

Later that day George received updates from his closest advisors. First through the door was Faith, who after some prevarication stated that the country was theologically sound and that George should maybe think of exporting some of his policies to the now occupied Greed.

"You know, Sir," he started, "there's always room for a little Faith alongside Greed and Repression."

"I'm not sure," said George. "if Repression will welcome Faith with open arms."

"Maybe not, Sir. They are, after all, Hopeless, but a little television never does anyone any harm." replied the crafty reverend.

George swatted a fly which had been buzzing around the two bottles in front of him.

"Creditcrisis says you have more money than Hope itself," said the thoughtful George. "It's time to make a tax deductable-donation."

"Sir, Faith doesn't pay taxes." replied the Reverend.

"Now you do," said George.

Faith left the meeting worried. Taxing Faith was dangerous. People should pay to pray he agreed, but the money must be used to expand Faith. Faith thought deeply. He decided a conversation with Reason was in order.

Back in his office, George had no idea the forces of Faith and Reason were about to find common ground. Faith and Reason, he giggled, who would think of such a pair?

General Disarray, besieged in Greed's capital, sent his envoy Miss Information to meet with George. Miss Information a tall long-legged woman, gave the mayor a glowing picture of activity on the ground.

"We are handing candy to starving children," she said proudly.

"What kind of candy?" asked George, hoping it wasn't the purple ones he liked so much.

"Oh, the syrupy ones which Faith produces," said Miss Information. "They spit most of it out, but some gets down."

"That Faith stuff is bad for the stomach," said George, "Gives me the willies!"

"Who said Faith was nice?" retorted Miss Information with a giggle.

George laughed as well. Being mayor could be fun.

Dick the Vice Mayor had been Turkey shooting in the north and arrived for his audience in military fatigues.

"Morning sir," said Dick.

"I like that uniform," said George. "Can you get me one?"

"Sure," said Dick. "My pleasure. They sell them at the Turkey Shop in Plunder."

George smiled, turning over a dead fly with his swatter.

"How's the country?" he asked nonchalantly.

"Don't really know," replied Dick, scratching his bald head.

"I've been thinking. Miss Information says they are handing out candy in Greed and they're goanna beam in television. Maybe we should vacation there. I'm tired of speedboats."

Dick was used to his boss's disconnected ideas and replied accordingly.

"No baseball, George, and flight tickets are hard to come by."

"Just a thought," replied George.

Generals Shock and Awe found George still toying with the dead fly. To amuse himself, the mayor had started flipping the fly in the air like a small pancake, catching it adroitly on the swatter, wondering why baseball players did not use swatters instead of bats.

"Well, Sir, another dose of Shock and Awe," said General Shock jovially.

"Well," said George. "I think we're handing out candy to the Hopeless. Maybe they'll come around."

"I doubt it, Sir," said Awe. "These people can't be civilized. We were hoping you would authorize a larger strike force so we could attack Want. Maybe we could bomb Need as well. Lord knows they need it."

George had not been paying the slightest bit of attention to the last sentence and without a bat of his eyelids turned to his Generals and said, "More baseball, that's what we need."

"Sir." began Shock carefully. "Greed is on the run, Want is contained but Peace doesn't stand a chance without money."

"Who's paying for the candy?" asked George.

"Faith," replied the Generals in unison.

Dr Creditcrisis was good at his job. Years of balancing unbalancable budgets, cutting funding and spiking water and energy prices had given almost God-like status within the administration. That was coupled with a singular lack of conscience which comes from believing he was smarter than everyone else.

But even he could not work miracles. On visiting the mayor that morning, he had unpleasant news.

"Sir, the country has no money."

George, who had discarded the unfortunate fly into a nearby trash can, was now searching for another unsuspecting victim.

"No money," he said. "What about my salary?"

"That's no problem, Sir." replied Creditcrisis. "We can simply print more money. What I mean is we have no money for education or health."

"Isn't everyone healthy?" inquired the curious George. "I thought we were a healthy country and wholesome, too. We play baseball, eat beef burgers, and watch television. That's healthy. Why do we need health care?"

"Oh, I agree." said Creditcrisis. "If a citizen's not healthy we shouldn't have to shoulder the expense. Same with education, I'll make the adjustments accordingly. That should buy us some time."

George was wondering about a world without money. Who would pay the baseball players? Sounded bad.

"I think," said George carefully. "that I'm going to have to take charge of spending."

Dr Creditcrisis looked at George and a thought crossed his mind.

"Sir, we could take all of Greed's money and not pay them for their Black Gold. Then the coffers would fill back up very quickly."

"Good idea," said George. "They don't need it anyway. They're getting free candy."

George was getting uncomfortable. He needed the toilet. Wriggling in his seat, he decided he had to go.

Dismissing Creditcrisis summarily, George skulked down the hallway in search of a bathroom. All were occupied however, so the stealthy Mayor stood outside the kitchen door and urinated onto the street.

The flash of a camera told George he was in trouble. A reporter from the local paper had caught our George, member in hand, pissing on the sidewalk.

"Sir," said the reporter, "any comments?"

"It wasn't me," said George hoping his oafish smile would convince the man.

The puddle of yellow urine which had collected on the sidewalk did not move, nor did it soak into the concrete and disappear. George looked at the puddle and then at the reporter. Rushing back inside the mayor's building, George was halfway down the hall before he realized he had not zipped his fly.

The newspapers seized upon George's misadventure. The morning headlines read, "George bears responsibility for people pissing in the street."

George took umbrage.

"This is a free country," he moaned to Big George. "I have a right to piss wherever I want."

"True," replied Big George. "But don't let people catch you doin' it."

George was about to admonish his father when he collected himself. He was tired of being Mayor anyway.

"I'm goanna resign," he said.

'That'll be hard," said Big George. "People prefer losers to quitters. Better just sleep out your term. Now on to more important things, son. What would you like for Christmas?"

"A new baseball set," answered George. "With the change strip as well and a new pair of cowboy boots with six inch heels. Boy, I need the toilet."

"Use the bathroom George," said Big George sternly.

Faith and Reason, emboldened by George's misdemeanor started unfolding their own plan. In searching for a replacement should George resign, they ran into trouble. Most of the citizens of Hope it appeared were as shallow if not shallower than George. Because of the cuts in education few could hold their own in any serious argument and most viewed political office as an albatross.

Their search produced three candidates each equally lacking. The most promising Slick Willie's long-suffering spouse, who had her personal axe to grind. Believing our George stood for bygone values and solutions she mercilessly attacked George's integrity and lack of intelligence.

Hope's citizens were subjected to a barrage of anti-George propaganda from the pulpit and in journals. The day seemed won when an extraordinary event occurred.

George's pet, Sheep Lucy, was run over in a large tank-like vehicle by the governor of a western province. The pitiful sight of George crying uncontrollably over Lucy's carcass touched the hearts of the populace who ultimately believed that George, whatever his shortcomings, displayed very ordinary emotions similar to their own.

His opponent furthered railroaded her case when she called George a cry baby, bubble-gum card loser.

So Faith and Reason made a difficult decision. For all his faults, George was a true representation of Hope's conscience. They decided to give him one last chance to mend his ways.

Thus we find George, friendless, advisorless and facing an ultimatum, sitting in his egg-shaped office playing with his new baseball set. George has tasted Faith and Temptation, mixing them into a dangerous cocktail and drinking his fill, but is finding he has no stomach for it.

His avid pursuit of Greed had lost him public support and war with Want loomed. Coupled with this, he was now perceived as insensitive to Need.

Does our George have more gumption? Hiding beneath his shallow exterior, is there a man willing to change?

We shall see soon because newly installed in his office are two phones. One a direct line to Shock and Awe, the other to his newly installed Secretary Reason. Which phone will George pick up?

What will George do next?

Fidei Defensor

"I'm not sure, Doctor," I said, stretching my legs closer to the fire. It crackled and seemed to beckon us closer.

My companion an ample, benign looking physician adjusted his spectacles. "Well, really my dear fellow, you must at least allow me to be the judge."

"Very well," I replied and added. "but you must remember that no offense is inferred or to be taken from my tale."

" None will be." said the doctor. "But before you start, let us at least make ourselves comfortable with some more of that excellent port."

The Doctor and I were sat in a walnut-paneled library. All light had been extinguished except the fire, which glistened off the port decanter on the center of the table that sat between us. We each filled our glasses and sat back in our leather arm chairs.

I removed my reading glasses, took a sip of port and began..

It was midway through the Michealmas term of 82 as I recall. I had been sometime previously summoned to the provost's office. After the usual niceties, he got down to business. Oriel he said still owned some land in East Anglia. One of the parishes was under the Rectorate of Horace Beaul, a former fellow of Oriel, Chaplain of Westminster School and contemporary of the provost's.

Beaul was a classicist of some renown. Amongst his best known works are the official translation of Athanasius' orations and a lengthy work on the early Greek fathers.

Beaul, the provost added had chosen to hide himself in this remote parish after retiring from academia, subsisting adequately on the living which he shared with the provost.

Recently, however, vandalism at a local abbey had uncovered certain manuscripts from the twelfth century, under the tomb of Sir Roger De Olivier, a knight best known for his participation in the taking of Jerusalem in 1093. The vandalism had attached some local attention, because on entering the crypt the vandals had inexplicably been crushed lifting the lid of De Olivier's sarcophagus.

Varying claims for ownership of the discovery had been submitted, but it was generally agreed that they required documenting first. Beaul, the foremost scholar in this area, was chosen to undertake the considerable task.

The sheer volume of these manuscripts had forced Beaul to ask for assistance from Oriel. As I was considered quite highly and had been raised locally, the provost had recommended me. For my part, I was only too happy to spend some time in the surroundings of my childhood, and the chance of working with Beaul was an opportunity too good to pass up.

Rural Essex is often forgotten and overlooked. It has, I suppose a rustic beauty and archaic charm, the small hamlets once so vital, the disused railway lines. It was to this area that I travelled in the autumn of 82 with my letter of introduction and certain nostalgia in my heart.

The village of which Beaul held the Rectorate was small. It had, I believe, no more than a thousand residents at any time. The centre, which included the church and rectory, was situated atop a small hill, as many religious sites in that area are.

The church was quaint, although somewhat decayed. It boasted a flinty fourteenth century tower with a magnificent view of the surrounding countryside. The devils door is mentioned in King's, 'Catholic antiquities in Anglican Essex.'

Next to the church on a slight incline sat the Rectory, a substantial building in Georgian style, with all the pomp and vastness which went with that period. It boasted a panoramic view of the surrounding countryside and some fine gardens. It was somewhat wasted on a single man.

Upon arrival at around midday, my host walked out in cassock and robe to greet me. He was a tall ruddy-faced man in his sixties with a full head of silver hair. His smile was full and his voice had an odd habit of carrying some distance.

He was, he said in the habit of taking a break from his studies at this hour and would I care to join him for lunch once I had unpacked? This I happily assented to and, within the hour, was sat opposite Beaul at a square dining room table enjoying a healthy repast of bread, tongue and salad. The room was largish even by Georgian standards, and walls were adorned with many period paintings which Beaul took care to describe to me.

"Well my boy." he jovially quipped once he had finished reviewing the artwork. "you're what the Provost has sent me, and I shall make good use of you."

During the meal, Beaul elaborated on the discovery made the previous year. The manuscripts had been secreted beneath the tomb of Sir Richard; most of them seem to recount the deceased knight's prowess, both physical and sexual, and even some of his thoughts on philosophy, as well as a clinical recounting of the first crusade.

This, Beaul pointed out, was not unusual for this time. Most Plantagenet's were extremely egocentric, and our heartless knight had also added the unusual term Defender of the Faith as suffix to his name, this some centuries prior to its adoption by the monarchy.

However, he added, along with these had been found some earlier Latin texts, not in Sir Richard's hand, and these were proving somewhat harder to decipher, although far more interesting.

Beaul proposed that I work on Sir Richard's recollections while he prepared the older documents.

"I must say," he said. "that I cannot pin-point their authorship. They appear pre-Nicene and yet almost clerical in their observations. I'm sure they are the work of one man."

After our lunch, Beaul walked me around the church and its adjoining land, pointing out anything of note to me.

The church and adjoining graveyard were wholly unmemorable and I see no need to describe them further here. After our walk I proceeded to the rectory library and, at Beaul's direction, began my preparing for my translations.

From what I read during the next week, I opined Sir Richard De Olivier to be particularly salacious individual with little or no care for his fellow man. His account of the brutality of the storming of Antioch was particularly blood thirsty, and several times I had to pause to take in the vileness of his tradition. It also was not beyond the devilish earl to pillage and plunder whatever antiquities he could find.

Beaul's personal library, which he had brought from Oxford, contained some background on Sir Richard. Our knight appeared a physically imposing man for his time, some six and a half feet tall and well-boned to boot. He had a large scar running down his right cheek and a severe limp, the result of wounds received during the final storming of Antioch.

The older documents that Beaul was translating were no doubt stolen by this reprobate with some hope to auction them for personal gain. Quite how this objectionable individual was ever allowed to couple himself with defense of the faith was beyond my comprehension.

Beaul and I spoke little on personal terms during this time. Most of our conversation centered on his documents and their mysterious authorship. They were, he said, observations of daily life in Judea and Cappadocia in or around the time of Christ. The Latin and Greek scripts were written by a man of some learning and considerable analytical powers. Once translated, he said, they would be sent for safe keeping to the British library.

One day, toward the end of my stay, Beaul summoned me to his study. He said that he wanted a younger man's opinion on a subject. I knocked and entered his study I noticed a change in his demeanor. He appeared vexed and somewhat dour. His spectacles he held in his right hand and, he chewed on one of the arms.

"What do you make of this?" he asked.

Gingerly I took the parchment he handed me. The Latin was barely visible through the layers of dust and dirt. I strained my eyes and read as best I could what was written.

"It appears," I said. "to be a testament or will, but I cannot openly translate."

Beaul appeared irritated. "I know what it is. That is my area of expertise. I mean, can you read the signature?"

I looked closely again, and then I realized it.

"John," I said. "John of Antioch, the Evangelist."

Beaul and I looked long and hard at each other. I do not know how much time passed.

"We have John's testament, great news." I said. Imagining the accolades that would follow, Beaul's place in history would be sealed and I would no doubt be asked to remain at Oxford as a fellow, my career set.

Beaul though did not appear happy. He had the same vexed expression on his face.

"There is something else I must confirm before we go any further. Shall we meet tomorrow? Let's say at ten in the vestry."

I did not argue, but thought it odd. Beaul knew I was not a religious man and he himself was really only a titular head of the parish. I went about my business anyway, not reflecting much on it. I was far to excited about the discovery of the document. I almost went as far as to cable the Provost but remembered Beaul had sternly warned me against any communication until the documents were completed.

The following morning at five minutes before ten I unlatched the church door. It was a large oak door, and it creaked at the slightest movement. Walking inside I found it empty. Waiting for Beaul, I looked over some of the artwork on the walls. I was just admiring a picture of a Semitic looking man in old Egyptian dress when behind me a voice boomed down the nave.

"It's Aaron, by Gertsa," said Beaul. Walking through the apse to the nave. I greeted him, and we shook hands.

"Morning, my boy," he said.

Again I was struck by how his voice carried. The acoustics of the empty church greatly augmented his voice.

"I must show you something." Without further ado, we entered the vestry. On the table was a small piece of parchment.

"Tell me," asked my host. "if you agree with my translation."It was in pencil on the edge of the parchment.

I read the document. It must have taken me sometime to register what I had read.

"This," I said to Beaul. "is a successor document."

He nodded. His eyes had become intense, I read out loud.

I bequeath my holdings to my lover Miriam and my son by that union. "

Signed this day .... The name on the parchment was faded but it was unmistakable. For a full two minutes I stared at the document and let the information sink in.

"My God," I said.

"My God, indeed," intoned Beaul.

We must, Beaul said take these immediately to the British library for verification. The implications he added were huge for mankind as a whole. Then he added, somewhat wryly, that he hoped they were a forgery.

The following day, Beaul had a service to give in a local church and I took the morning off. I arrived back to the Rectory at one to find Beaul outside pacing up and down. He had an odd expression on his face. He said the documents were gone,

"All of them/" I asked.

"No. Just the testament." he moaned. "I have lost it."

After consoling Beaul, I investigated his study, but found nothing untoward. Neither a leaf nor book was out of place. The documents appeared to have vanished into thin air, perhaps I opined my host had become absent minded. A clinical search of the grounds also proved fruitless.

We reported the theft of the documents, although not their content to the local police, who were to say the least somewhat skeptical. On account of Beaul's standing a full investigation was undertaken which included scouring local book stores and antique dealers, but the documents never showed up. I must admit it had crossed my mind that Beaul had destroyed them in a fit of religious zeal.

"Not much of a ghost story," laughed the Doctor.

"Not really." I agreed. "But, allow me to finish."

"Finish, you shall," said my companion.

"Well, here's the odd thing. During the police investigation, Beaul's housekeeper, Mrs. Slee was questioned. She was of honest rustic stock and the cloud of suspicion never fell on her. She did however have one strange contribution to make. When asked if any strangers had been seen around the Rectory that day she replied in the negative, but when pressed sometime later revealed an interesting fact. She had let the postman in that day for glass water. It had not apparently been the usual man that day, but a rather odd fellow she said some six or more feet tall with a scar on his left cheek and dreadful limp!"

At that moment, Dr Silverman bade me stop. "Have some more port old chap." he said. "I think I've heard enough."

Let There Be Light

Adjusting his suspenders to hold up his trousers up, Marvin Jacobson peered around the cracked barn door into the night. It was dark outside and the light inside the barn made night vision difficult. Screwing up his eyes, Marvin looked again.

"Nothing," he said, closing the barn door gingerly. "I think we're in the clear...

He walked back to the center of the barn where five other men sat on straw bales. Taking his seat on an empty one, he drew his sleeve across his perspiring brow.

The men Marvin sat with were all similar looking to him, stocky and in their mid fifties. Each wore an open necked shirt and casual pants, although Marvin was the only one with suspenders.

Marvin Jacobson cleared his throat and pulled up his suspenders. He looked at each of his companions, the steady gaze of his eyes seeming to read their thoughts.

"This," he said with a resigned expression on his face. "May be the last time we meet."

Five heads looked at him and nodded in agreement.

Changing his position on one of the bales, a man named Alan said, "We are all grateful to you, Marvin, for calling this meeting."

Marvin nodded, acknowledging the thanks.

Alan continued,

"Things are getting worse. The Theological Police are everywhere now! Even my own wife suspects me of being an atheist. I don't think she'll turn me in, but one never knows. "

"It's those damn 'may the lord be with yous,'" added a second man.

Everyone nodded in agreement.

"We have to disband. They suspect too much already." said Alan

"That's why I called this meeting." said Marvin. "We can't meet anymore, but we still must spread the word as we did before."

"How can we?" asked another man. "How do you recognize another atheist?"

Alan stood up, dust rising from the bale of hay under him. He thrust his hand into his pockets and spoke.

"We need to be able to identify ourselves to each other." he said. Then as an afterthought he added. "Any ideas?"

"How about a hand signal?" suggested one fellow.

"Too obvious." said Alan.

"Besides," added Marvin, "Freemasons use that. None of use wants to be up on a Freemasons charge. That's at least a year's worth of treatment."

" I think," said Alan, "that we should use a phrase that the Theological Police could not pick up on, a religious phrase maybe."

Several of the group murmured. A taller man whose name was Bert stood up and adjusted his glasses.

"We are Atheists," he said defiantly. "We do not and will not use religious phrases! It's against the founding code."

"Look where the founding code has gotten us," replied Alan. "We are six. We used to be hundreds."

"Let's vote on it," suggested another man.

Everyone nodded and Marvin stood up and asked for all in favor and against. The Yeas had it four to two, and Marvin, with a rush of inspiration, said.

"Let there be light, that's our phrase. Let there be light. There's nothing religious about that."

Everyone nodded, even the reluctant Bert, and the motion passed. The meeting broke up soon afterwards, and the men said their goodbyes hoping to meet again sometime in the future.

Marvin lived with his wife of fifteen years. It had been a happy marriage for the most part until five years ago. The religious revolution which had taken hold in the twenties had accelerated its grip on power and Marvin's wife had become a convert.

Marvin, a staunch atheist since adolescence, had not complained at first, believing that the country was going through a phase. He was wrong. Within a year a religious party was in power and, using a little known constitutional clause, had extended their power indefinitely. On the surface it seemed somewhat benign but every day brought a tightening of restrictions if you did not ascribe to the state faith.

The state faith, a form of evangelical Protestantism, had started out as an obscure rural religion, but emboldened by power and with a dogma that appealed to the masses, it had gained ground quickly. Soon it obliterated or absorbed all other Christian sects and encouraged the forcible conversions or expulsions of non-Christians.

The faith however had a larger target. While acknowledging the rights of other states to pursue other faiths, it drew the line at atheism. Calling it a world wide cancer, small but malignant. It mercilessly pursued its foe. The government's law enforcement wing, the Theological Police was given the job of enforcing the anti-atheism policy. By the time Marvin Jacobson was forty the government claimed to be winning the war against atheism.

A year or so later Marvin and his friend Alan had founded the atheist movement that had met the previous night. It never boasted a membership greater than a hundred, most people being too scared to take part. Two years ago the government had announced a clamp down on atheism hoping to eradicate it by years end. The result had been a heightened state of paranoia. Friends and relatives handed over information both true and false to the religious authorities.

The result was that Marvin Jacobson's little group dwindled to six.

The punishment for atheism was increased from three to six months internment in religious camp. Religious camp was a detention centre in which the unfortunate inmate was subject to a rigorous regimen of bible classes and scriptural dissertation. Few who went in ever wanted to go back.

The Theological Police force whose job it was to enforce the religious laws of the state was made up mainly of over zealous converts or second generation faith elders who pursued their tasks with a single-mindedness befitting of their positions. The consequence of all this being that most atheists hid their beliefs so well, that even close family members were unaware of them.

Marvin Jacobson's wife had become a victim of conversion early on. The constant television programs and faith based government departments had resigned her to a, "if you can't beat them join them" attitude. She had been a card carrying church member for four years.

Marvin himself had lived in the shadows keeping himself very much to himself. His daily toil at a retail outlet did not put him into daily contact with the Theological Police and if it ever should, thanks to his wife, he knew enough jargon to get by.

Ten years ago Marvin had been approached by Alan Kerridge. He had rebuffed most of the approaches, claiming no knowledge of atheism or its practices and even once threatening to call the authorities on Alan. However Alan Kerridge was a persistent man and after several weeks Marvin had agreed to join the Atheist club that Alan had founded some years previously.

They had both been active in it since, but as the conversation at the last meeting foretold, it was a losing battle. The numbers had dwindled and now they had agreed to disband and talk to each other in private, one-on-one when possible.

Five years or so after the last meeting, Marvin was at work in his store when a young man walked in. Clean cut and with a happy-go-lucky manner, he busied himself looking at the merchandise.

"May the lord be with you," he greeted Marvin with the State's official form of address.

"And with you, too," replied Marvin without hesitation.

"Can I help you?" inquired Marvin

The young man hummed a little hymn and looked directly at Marvin. Marvin did not like the gaze and turned his head away scratching his ear at the same time.

"Let there be light," said the young man.

Marvin Jacobson had been given good perceptive skills and he sensed falseness to the man using his codeword, but he was also inquisitive enough to need an explanation. He chose his words carefully.

"Do you seek light?" he asked, inside congratulating himself on the obscurity of the sentence.

"I think I do," replied the young man staring right back at him. "I was told that this is where I might find it."

"Who told you that?" snapped back Marvin, now feeling and looking nervous.

"A man who gave me water when I was injured," said the young man.

Marvin Jacobson decided to stop right there. His nerves had gotten the better of him and he told the young man he could be of no assistance. The young man simply stared at him and smiled. He bought a cheap packet of glue and walked out, bidding Marvin a good day.

On arriving home that night, Marvin's wife greeted him and over dinner told him of some visitors she had that afternoon. She described two older men in their sixties, working class types who had come looking for him. They said they had been sent by a man with whom they worked several years ago.

"They kept on repeating, 'Let there be light,'" she said.

Marvin said nothing but sat down, a drained look on his face. "This is it," he thought. "The Theological Police have finally found me and they are going to hound me until I confess. Then a year in religious camp...Oh no!" he thought.

Walking over to the drinks cabinet he poured himself a large scotch and downed it. Then another, then another.

"What's the matter?" asked his wife.

Marvin Jacobson did not answer his wife, for at that moment he believed everyone was after him. He downed another scotch and went upstairs to bed. The alcohol took effect and Marvin passed into sleep believing he would be woken halfway through the night and hauled off to religious camp.

Marvin awoke with a headache the next morning, but still in his own bed. He took sometime getting up, still expecting a knock on the door from the Theological Police. His wife avoided him and Marvin headed to work as usual.

Getting out of his car Marvin started to unlock his store when out of the corner of his eye he noticed the same young man from the previous day sitting on an upturned trash can across the street. Upon seeing Marvin he rose and crossed the road.

"Let there be light," he said again, a huge smile on his face. Marvin noticed he was wearing the same clothes.

Marvin ignored him and walked into his store. Switching on the lights and altering a few displays he hoped the man would go away. When he hung the open sign outside, he noticed the young man was still there.

It was then that Marvin did something completely irrational. Opening the door he beckoned the young man to come in. Hanging the closed sign up, he took him into the back room with a table and chairs and invited him to sit down.

The young man thanked him and said. "Do you know the way to the light?"

"Who are you?" Marvin asked.

"My name is James," said the young man.

"Explain to me again why you are here." asked Marvin.

"The man who helped me when I was injured, as I already told you," said James.

"Tell me more." said Marvin.

James went on to recount that a year ago he had been in a traffic accident. The Theological Police had arrived at the scene and determined him to have been speeding. This being the case, the scripture called for him to be held accountable, and, after towing his vehicle, they left him by the side of the road to die, as the law called for.

"I was delirious with pain and ready to receive my maker's judgment when an older man stopped his car at great personal risk and said to me, "Let there be light.""

James coughed slightly, placed his hands on the table and continued his story.

"Well, I did not know what the man meant so I said, 'Let there be light' back. The man gave me water and some medicine. He came back that night and loaded me in his car and drove me to a hospital. He told them I had been injured accidently, and they treated me. I never saw him again..."

"Where did you learn my name?" asked Marvin, still a might suspicious.

"During the car journey to the hospital, I thanked him and asked him about the light. He said if I needed more information I should contact a man named Marvin who had originated the search for light."

"Are you a policeman?" asked Marvin.

James face went white. He stammered his reply.

"No. No." he replied How could you think such a thing? I seek the light, not the darkness and the old ways."

Marvin looked at the young man sitting opposite the table from him. He did not seem to be a member of the Theological Police. Marvin was puzzled and needed time to think.

"Come back tomorrow," said Marvin and he saw his visitor out.

When he arrived home that day there was a car in his driveway. Marvin half thought to turn round and go back to the store, but his inquisitiveness got the better of him. Parking his car behind the strange vehicle, he headed hastily for his front door.

Opening his front door, he walked in. In his living room saw his wife entertaining two older men. Both stood up when Marvin entered the room. Marvin took stock of the men. Both appeared to be working men, in their late fifties maybe.

"Who are these people?" he asked his wife.

"Let there be light," said one of the men looking directly at Marvin

Marvin sank down in his sofa and loosened his tie. "So this is it," he thought "They have come to get me. No use in resisting." He sat still waiting for one of them to arrest him. Instead, to Marvin's surprise, his wife started telling him what they had told her.

"Marvin, these people got your name from a man who helped them once at work. He told them if they ever needed more information they should seek you out and ask about the light. I told them I didn't know what they were talking about, but they refused to leave."

"Are you from the state?" asked Marvin.

"Not at all," replied one of the men in a rural accent.

Marvin was thinking quickly to himself, "Alan must have got around in the last few years. I wonder how many people like this he had spoken to". For the first time in the last few days Marvin felt relieved and let out a large laugh. The men looked at him quizzically.

Inviting the men to stay for dinner, Marvin listened intently to their stories. The first had been on the verge of committing suicide, a mortal sin, when Alan had come into his life and persuaded him that things were not so bad. Frequent conversations with Alan had allowed the man to regain his self confidence, and within several weeks his suicidal thoughts had disappeared.

The second fellow, hounded by his own inadequacy, saw no future in faith, but Alan had persuaded him a greater light existed and could be achieved by even those of modest intellect.

Listening closely Marvin Jacobson began to get an idea. It was not original, but one that had its seeds in the final meeting years ago. Only now it was forming and taking shape. Try though he might, Marvin could not get rid of the thought. All the time and effort he had spent on atheism had gone unrewarded. By the end of the evening, his company gone and wife asleep, Marvin was still thinking.

The following morning the three men stood outside Marvin's store as he opened it. Letting them in they all proceeded to the back room. There the two older men admitted there were more of them who sought Marvin.

"At least ten that I know," he said.

"And I know of thirty more." added James. "Let's bring them along, Marvin, for they too seek the light."

Marvin Jacobson was a practical man but also suspicious.

"What about the Theological Police?" he asked.

"What about them?" answered James, shrugging his shoulders. "It's not like we're atheists."

The quartet laughed out loud together, Marvin's eyes narrowed somewhat and he brought the meeting to order.

Immanuel's First Piano Lesson

The sun was setting on that golden September afternoon, and the man seated at the table in the garden appeared tired. The man, whose name was Immanuel had been deep in thought for most of the day, carefully taking stock of the scenery and activity around him. He coughed and reached a the decanter of wine in the centre of the table. The libation relaxed him and he looked to the papers in his hand, studying them looking for errors, but finding none. Then, as had been custom for many years, he stretched out in his chair and thought. He was a deep thinker, he had been since childhood, and he let his mind wander over his deductions and slowly drifted into a light sleep.

In front of him there sat an older man. The man was bald and wore an open-necked shirt. He helped himself to a glass of wine, briefly holding it up as if to toast Immanuel.

Immanuel grinned wryly his gaze moving quickly from his visitor to a clump of holly trees to his left, their sharp leaves cutting the light in geometric perfection.

"Well," said Immanuel to his visitor, "I hope you are satisfied?"

"Satisfied? Yes," said his visitor. "But I would clarify one point."

"Yes?" said Immanuel. His gaze now directed on his companion.

The older man stood up and stared upward at the higher branches of the fir trees which surrounded the glade area in which they sat. "I need to be sure that it cannot be reasoned otherwise."

"It cannot," said Immanuel emphatically.

"Very well," said his companion. "Then it is done." Once again he raised his glass to Immanuel.

It was the sound of his own voice assuring his companion that awakened Immanuel that September afternoon. That and the distant sound of a piano drifting through the early evening air.

The sun slowly faded on that golden September afternoon and Immanuel listened to the sound of a piano playing somewhere in the distance, its melody distant but audible to him as he rubbed his eyes. He had heard the piano every afternoon at this time for the last three years, yet on this particular day, he sought its origins. Heading out of the garden, Immanuel walked quickly toward the river which flanked the garden and across a wooden bridge.

On the far side was a steep embankment with a thin path that cut the incline like a flowing ribbon, and Immanuel started up it. It was a hard climb, but Immanuel attacked it like a man possessed. His determination over rode any discomfort he felt from the nettles which abounded on the hillside.

Beyond the crest of the embankment stood a small wooden cottage. He walked in its direction, first slowly then faster, hurrying as if believing himself late for something.

The cottage was small, the roof thatched and large flowers overgrew the small pathway leading to the front door. Immanuel walked straight down the pathway following the music his legs brushing the unkempt plantings and unlatched the front door without knocking.

He entered into a small living area reminiscent of his own dwelling. The room was sparsely decorated, just a table with chairs and there was a smell of marigolds. Immanuel dusted himself off as he entered the dead pollen and dust hanging in the evening light.

A middle-aged women sat playing a piano in the center of the room. She was dark with classical features; her chestnut hair fell easily on her shoulders. She looked up at Immanuel as he entered the room. Her expression surprised him it was as if she knew he was coming.

Immanuel stood in the centre of the room staring intently at the woman at her keyboard, she returned his gaze. He started to ask a question, then stopped, as if wanting to rephrase it, but after some thought started again

"Of what do you think?" asked Immanuel without bothering to introduce himself. "What do think of when you play that tune?" Immanuel was only vaguely aware he was repeating himself.

The woman appeared to anticipate the question. Without much thought and barely looking up from her keyboard she replied, "I think of a circle of trees." After a moment, she added, "I'm stood in the middle of a perfect circle of trees, looking up at a crystal clear cloudless sky."

Her fingers moved gently over the keys, her head swaying with the music.

Immanuel seemed astonished. He paused, thought and then mumbled.

"Then it's true, but it cannot be, it cannot be." He looked ashen as if something he had been seeking his whole life had suddenly been revealed to him.

"My dear man," said the woman, "you've gone quite pale."

Immanuel moved over toward the fire place, which was on the far wall. There was a small arm-chair made out of dark wood. He sat down, his stare never leaving the piano and the woman sat at it. His face twisted as if in torment. Immanuel put his hands together as if to ease his thought, after sometime he asked another question.

"When you play that piece do you seek perfection?" he asked.

"I do," replied the woman. "But I do with all my pieces," she added.

"Is it perfect?" asked Immanuel sharply, as if knowing the answer.

"To me, yes," replied he woman. "Why, what a lot of questions you have."

"And," continued Immanuel, as if speaking to someone outside the room, "if you played it again, would it still be perfect?"

The fire crackled. Immanuel did not hear it.

"I do not know," admitted the pianist. "I would however strive to perfection." She looked right at him, curious to know what was on his mind.

Immanuel did not move. He closed his eyes envisioning...

.....Two people on separate banks of a river unknown to each other both simultaneously seeking perfection in one thought. If the thoughts are imperfect, reasoned Immanuel, the sum would be perfect.....If they both construed the same thought at the same time then that is perfect... a perfect match....Therefore he reasoned all things must begin in perfection....a perfect condition....

He also saw a man stood by a column, dressed in a white robe pointing to a large circle he had drawn in the sand below. The man appeared to be telling him something, maybe that he had drawn a perfect circle maybe that he could not draw it.

At this point, Immanuel's eyes opened and he requested his companion play the music again.

The woman looked long and deeply at Immanuel. She smiled and her visitor smiled back. Starting at the beginning the pianist repeated the allegro.

Again, Immanuel closed his eyes and verbalized his thoughts to his companion." the trees are tall; equal in height...They are differing shades of green. They form a..."

"Perfect Circle," ended the pianist.

Immanuel already knew this would happen.

"We are thinking the same thought." he said.

The woman did not reply, her eyes fastened on the keyboard.

"When you wrote this piece what or whom did you have in mind?" asked Immanuel

"You," replied the woman. "I see you daily sat in the garden on the other side of the river and long......

"To speak to me." Immanuel ended her sentence.

Something had shattered in Immanuel's mind. He closed his eyes once again drawing comfort from the peace he found in blackness. His thoughts ran long and deep, yet he could not get the melody the woman had been playing out of his head. The dancing allegro played in his mind, bouncing off his inner thoughts and bringing back full circle again to the face of the pianist. When he opened his eyes he realized he had been incorrect.

"How long have you listened to me?" asked the pianist tossing back her chestnut hair, her fine features more evident as the light faded.

"I don't know," admitted Immanuel. "A long time I think."

"Then how did you imagine me?" asked the pianist.

Immanuel still with the look of a man who has just had something revealed to him took a moment to answer.

"Almost the way you are." he said.

Smiling longingly at the pianist, he walked over to the piano and bent his head, she raised hers at the same time and they kissed.

As he drew his head away they smiled simultaneously. Immanuel promised to return the following day and he left.

On the footpath leaving her cottage he could hear the piano through the open windows. The music drifted lightly on the summer air. Immanuel fancied the music to be following him down the embankment to the river bridge, where the embankment ended.

Immanuel walked home a thoughtful man that night. He stopped many times on his short journey as if reasoning deeply in his head, and at times he closed his eyes and smiled.

Late into the night Immanuel wrote. He went through more than one candle. Sat writing, he longed to speak to his visitor of the previous afternoon to tell him there was an error. As he wrote he imagined the pleasures that awaited him in the cottage across the river, the endless nights of perfection and complement.

But alas wisdom is poor if the wise do not profit from it. Something else was in store for Emmanuel. As morning came he drifted into a deep sleep, the parchment slipped from his hand and fell into the fire place, lighting up briefly in a beautiful amber flame before the fire consumed it.

Kant's proof of God had been lost to time.....

Life Commitment

Sometimes the last thing people do is make a commitment. Simon Gurney had difficulty making commitments. In fact, his life had been plagued by a lack of them. Stuck in a dead end job and living in a less than desirable neighborhood, he was a classic no-hoper. Simon was in love with the woman opposite him that day and had been for the last year. He had, in different meetings over the past year of his life, confided his darkest feelings and shared his most intimate secrets with her.

The woman whose name was Ruth Black was aware of Simon's feelings and for a good part she returned them, but now a pivotal moment in the relationship had arrived. They were sitting in her living room, she in a comfortable armchair and he on a leather seat. Both were casually dressed, although she a lot trendier than he.

Running her tongue inside her top lip purposely to produce a sensual effect on Simon, she spoke quietly. Her voice had a New York brogue to it.

"Simon, I just cannot keep on doing what you ask," she said. "I must have a commitment."

Simon Gurney wriggled as if he were a small mouse. He was giving in slowly.

"What more do you want, Ruth? I've signed half my savings over to you. Surely, that is enough of a commitment."

Ruth smiled. This was getting difficult. She crossed her legs, a sign of denial. Simon eyed the knee length boots.

"Simon I don't need money; I need a commitment," she repeated.

Silence reigned in the room. Ruth could almost hear Simon Gurney thinking. Standing up to reveal her well-proportioned physique, she took her jacket off. Underneath she wore a tight white shirt that clung to her breasts. Today she was going to have to get inventive.

Simon Gurney had met Ruth by chance in a hotel bar late one night. They both had been drinking far too much and he was attracted to her no-nonsense intelligence. They booked a room later that night and natural desires had taken over.

For Simon, it was enjoyable. He was one of those men who had a distinct inferiority complex when it came to women. But Ruth had allayed all those fears, and by the end of the first encounter Simon was hopelessly in love.

He did not, however, know how Ruth felt about him, and he decided, upon her suggestion to give their relationship a year. So, for the next year they saw each other three times a week. Simon could barely contain his excitement. They always met in her flat downtown. The flat was neatly decorated with the eye of a perceptive woman, comfortable and relaxed, with a trace of cold efficiency.

One of Simon's biggest hang-ups from childhood was sexual deviance. He liked to be dominated in a sensual way, and in Ruth he found a willing partner. The weekly dates, which always took place on the same days, were full of erotic foreplay and sexually explicit conversation.

Ruth knew what Simon Gurney desired. Frequently dressing in short skirts with long leather boots to tease and torment while she asked Simon to reveal his greatest desires on the leather chair opposite her.

Most dates ended with torrid intercourse on the floor, and although Simon thought it odd they never used the bed, he did not mind. He preferred the feel of the carpet on his back as he struggled underneath her.

Six months or so into their relationship, Ruth had surprisingly proposed marriage. Simon was uneasy, for much as he imagined himself in love with her, he did not like commitments. He refused and Ruth was so displeased she said she did not wish to see him again.

A week without Ruth was too much for the hapless Simon to bear, and he came sniveling back. Ruth, receiving him as usual in her lounge, sat him down. Dressed for his pleasure she rubbed a riding crop along her boots. Simon drooled.

"Sit down," she commanded.

Simon sat down.

"Undress," Her voice was harsh yet sensual, and Simon did as he was told. "And lie down on the floor," she added.

Then sitting astride him she explained that things were going to be different from now on. He needed to realize that for the relationship to continue, he was going to have to commit. She rolled the letters off her tongue slowly.

Simon was scared of commitment, so his mind quickly worked a compromise. Like most men who have been single most of their lives, Simon had amassed a large amount of capital. To prove his earnestness in the relationship, he said he would transfer these funds to a joint account as security for Ruth. If the relationship were to end, she would be entitled to half his life's savings.

Ruth seemed satisfied, although she told him honestly that she made a fair living and was not impoverished. Sitting astride him, she warned him that he was ultimately going to have to make a greater commitment than that. Simon nodded.

Simon though, was happy and happier still over the next six months when he found much to his surprise that Ruth had not touched the money in the account, in fact she had even added a little.

During the next months, Ruth provided Simon Gurney with sexual pleasure he could previously only find in magazines. Her dominatrix personality completely unfettered, she drove poor Simon wild.

Toward the end of the year, she once again asked Simon to sign a commitment, and again Simon refused.

Sat opposite him that day, her eyes bored into him. Her leather boots chaffed and rubbed against each other. Letting her glasses slip to the end of her nose, she peered over them seductively at Simon.

"Do you want me to bind and gag you?" she asked, running her tongue around her lips.

Simon nodded dumbly, and within a minute Ruth sat astride him and had his feet and left arm bound. Sitting astride him she moved her boots against his thighs. Simon made a face.

"Simon, I understand you do not want to get married," she said.

Simon's mind was on other things. His eyes closed tight, and his toes wriggled.

"Do we have to go through this again?" asked Simon.

"No" said Ruth. "I've drawn up some papers on the table there. They are a legal commitment, not a marriage license application."

Simon said he was not sure he understood.

"It's just a commitment. Look." Rising off the bound Simon, Ruth walked over to the table and picked up the papers. Remounting Simon, she showed him a large paper with a word that looked like "commitment" written in large black print.

Simon Gurney, in a heightened stage of sexual arousal, agreed to sign. Ruth took a pen from her shirt pocket. Grinding her hips and digging her heels, she gave Simon the pen and he signed.

That day, Simon experienced the best sexual act he ever had, and to heighten his pleasure Ruth told him she would leave him bound while she went out for a few hours.

Simon lay there for an hour or two. Some of the time he nodded off. Ruth had restrained him well, and he had difficulty moving. So to pass the time he decided to masturbate.

Two hours later two admitting nurses from the New York state asylum arrived back at the flat with court signed committal papers. They were accompanied by Doctor Ruth Green, physician on call. The admitting nurses found Simon Gurney naked on his Psychiatrists living room floor, tied up and masturbating.

"This one's really barmy." said the first nurse.

Ludwig and the Perennial Gardener

Ludwig had spent his life looking for perfection. In every flower, tree, river anything natural he sought the ultimate. As soon as he believed he had found it, another better example caught his attention.

Ludwig was also very conceited, considering himself more intelligent than his fellow man. He added to this a bad habit of enjoying menial jobs. This, he reasoned, was because he had a need to relate to simple things. He neglected to mention that at the menial level no one questioned his thought processes and that, due to a substantial inheritance, he had the means to engage in such pursuits.

Centuries ago the Benedictine brothers had sought sanctuary in the Tyrolean Mountains, believing the isolation and altitude would bring them closer to God. They built a stone monastery in small valley well up into the main range. It had started out as a simple affair but over time had grown larger. The monks had taken care to blend it in with the surrounding country; subsequently the landscape would now have looked incomplete without it.

Ludwig had been a gardener at the monastery for many months. He had sought out its solitude and simplicity, believing that this would help him solve the philosophical problems with which he wrestled daily and that had so long eluded him.

Ludwig had been given the job of planting new bulbs. In each new bulb he planted, he perceived greater perfection. His obsession for was never satisfied. So much so that it seemed never ending.

There were employed at this monastery several other gardeners. The Abbot had given each a particular task. Most were locals who had worked at the monastery most of their lives. They congregated at break time in a small shed behind the main rose gardens. The shed was small, the inside ringed with shelves that held badly stacked pots and bags of fertilizer. The floor covered with a thin coat of soil which filled the air with dust upon contact.

The gardeners did not take their break at the same time; they were coupled together in half-hourly intervals. Ludwig was paired with an older man who took care of the perennials which grew in the lower borders opposite the refectory.

Ludwig did not like the man, believing him both ignorant and stupid. The perennial gardener, whose name was Johannes thought Ludwig both conceited and a bad gardener. For the first month of Ludwig's employment they did not speak to one another choosing make their thoughts known by motioning crudely at one another. After this period they began to communicate by making abstract comments about the weather and foliage.

However much to Ludwig's annoyance, Johannes followed most of his general comments with the words "God willing." Ludwig, who did not suffer fools gladly, had been itching for sometime to challenge this comment, and Johannes, believing Ludwig to be a godless creep, was only too keen to engage him on the topic.

One morning, by chance, they found themselves working the upper rosecae together. It was a pleasant spring morning, and the smell of flowers encouraged the two protagonists to take their breaks outside by a barrow. Johannes took off his cap and sat down, perspiring on the top of an overturned barrow which had been used to prepare peat. Ludwig, taking the cue from the older man, perched himself atop another overturned barrow.

"God," started Johannes, giving a sweeping look over the vast plantage in front of him, "has given us this beautiful day." He wiped his brow on the arm of the cotton shirt he wore.

This comment found an eager recipient in Ludwig, who had spent some time waiting to hear a challenging or provocative comment from Johannes. His interest was doubly piqued because the two men were alone. Ludwig imagined himself momentarily as a circus master, taming a particularly vicious lion. He figured, however, to toy with this insolent fellow a while.

Scratching his nose with his fore-finger, he paused before asking, "What is God?" There was a certain sneer to his tone.

"That which is greater than I." Johannes said without wasting any time.

Ludwig was not in the mood for primitive answers, which he considered beneath him.

"Other people are greater than you, but you do not give them such a name," Ludwig said, grinning for good measure. This was going to be fun, he thought.

Johannes looked at Ludwig askance, as one would stare at an onion in a rose patch. He had expected this day to come, and Ludwig had stated something that Johannes had known and he had been waiting for.

"Not greater," he replied.

He then looked Ludwig directly in the eye. Ludwig had a feeling the fellow was looking right through him and briefly had a feeling of complete transparency.

"Although some would be as arrogant as to suppose they are," added Johannes his cold stare fixed on Ludwig.

"Semantics, again," said Ludwig, convinced the argument was over before it had begun. He also doubted the gardener understood the word. Ludwig stood up to emphasize his point...

"My good fellow," continued Ludwig, a nasal twang in his tone. "Let me start by explaining that the world is everything and that is the case." He followed his words with an imperious stare.

Johannes disregarded Ludwig's comment completely, and focusing on his companions' initial question answered again, "That which is true," he said.

"I'm true," said Ludwig, smirking. In the distance, the sun moved momentarily behind a cloud, giving the two protagonists a moment's respite from the warm mountain day.

The cloud seemed to throw a little different ambience on the pair.

"I don't know what you say is true. Only God does." replied Johannes sharply. It was quick retort and Ludwig wasn't expecting it.

"NO, I KNOW MYSELF," shouted Ludwig.

Ludwig's face reddened, how dare this insolent fellow suppose he did not know what truth was. If only he had half a brain he would tell him who he really was, but he thought the better of it.

"You think you know, but what if your logic deceives you?" inquired Johannes.

The comment elicited a visible change from Ludwig. For the first time during the conversation, he was forced to spend some time thinking of a reply. When he replied it was with great skill.

"I know it does not," he said, with finality in his voice that only he comprehended.

"Then you presume yourself God, and my point is made," replied the old man who took care of the perennials.

"Something must be greater than you, because you are not perfect," Johannes said decisively, knowing he was winning the argument.

Ludwig had a look of exasperation on his face and an irritation he had not experienced since arguing in a university many years previously. Then, as if to conclude the argument and accept a draw he blurted out.

"Your career belies your intellect."

"So does yours," answered the old gardener, as if he had waited for this moment his whole life.

The late morning sun reappeared from behind the cloud bank, and the two men went back to work. Ludwig dug with a newfound vigor, and Johannes continued on as before.

Some years later at Cambridge, after giving a lecture on absolutes, language and their places in the human consciousness, Ludwig was engaged by a young and intense student.

"Professor," she said, "I'm still not convinced. We all must have absolutes to live by."

"Young lady," Ludwig replied, his nasal twang evident and giving her the same imperious gaze he had given Johannes years previously. "here is a paradox for you."

For the first time since she had arrived at Cambridge the student caught a little humility in the rigid Austrian's voice.

"There are no absolutes," he continued, "but Professor Wittgenstein absolutely hates gardening!!!!!"

Arcadia Comes of Age

Weekly executions were a popular event in the town of Ravensberg, giving the rustic townspeople a regular entertainment to look forward to, and distance themselves from life's problems. The gallows, a rudimentary affair made of forest oak had solemnly done its duty for many years, providing a source of income for the executioner and entertainment for the townspeople.

The executioner, a short, stout fellow in his forties from a local village, was experienced at his trade, having some two hundred successful hangings to his name.

On this particular Monday, the condemned men were three gypsies. Two had been convicted of sheep stealing and the punishment was considered cruel even by the blood-thirsty townsfolk. The third gypsy, just eighteen years old, had been found guilty of several violent rapes and murders in the area and his execution was to bring to an end an unhappy chapter in local history.

The three convicted men stood on the platform blind-folded, their hands bound behind their backs. The crowd, some thirty strong cheering and jeering mostly from the effects of alcohol waited impatiently for the sentence to be carried out. The town crier announced the men's names and the crimes for which they were to receive the ultimate punishment. Then the executioner pulled the lever, and the sentence was carried out.

The three bodies hung for an hour, necks broken, eyes staring in astonishment at the now departed crowd.

Sure that everyone had left, the executioner and his assistant, a small chubby woman also in her forties cut down and loaded the first two bodies onto the death cart. Before loading the third, the executioner reached inside the trousers of the suspended man. Taking a knife, he sliced inside and removed a small cloth bag that had been strung low on the man's waist. Wrapping it quickly and giving it to his assistant, he cut down and loaded the third body onto the cart. When they were done he nodded at his assistant who headed toward the town on foot. He mounted the cart, shook the reins and headed in the opposite direction. The horse pulling the cart broke into a trot. Urging the horse to greater speed, the executioner joined the main road out of town.

Two miles down the road was a small gypsy encampment. Pulling over by its entrance the executioner was greeted solemnly by four young men, swarthy and dark, their eyes full of suspicion. The tallest spoke to the executioner.

"You have brought back our dead I see."

The executioner nodded and indicated the three corpses in the rear of the cart. The gypsies off loaded them, muttering sadly under their breaths, tears welling up in their eyes. The executioner waited, tapping his foot against the cart wheel, his horse periodically snorting. Once they had finished, he removed his hat and followed the sad group toward the center of the camp.

A small wake had assembled by one of the caravans, brightly dressed women, head scarves hiding their despondence, men looking out of place in dress coats, unshaven and sun-burned.

As the executioner awaited payment for transporting the bodies, a gypsy women no more than forty years in age approached him.

Pointing at him she said. "You, did you plead his case as you said you would?"

"I did," replied the executioner.

"So young," said the woman, her dark eyes flicking over the corpse of the third gypsy.

"His brothers were good boys, but he was so young and troubled," said another woman her eyes flashing as she spoke.

"The judge told me that being disturbed is no excuse for murder," answered the executioner.

An elder male gypsy came from out of one of the caravans and pressed a pouch into the executioner's hand. The executioner nodded in deference and made to leave.

But before he could make his way out a small commotion erupted behind him. One of the men, it appeared, had noticed that the youngest victim's trousers were sliced. Shouting curses at the executioner, he had to be restrained by the other men.

"What have you done?" yelled the gypsy his arms reaching around his restraints and toward the executioner. "Defiled him even in death? You will pay."

"Stand back now," said the executioner, swiftly drawing a pistol from his pocket. "Or I'll shoot you all like dogs."

There was a momentary standoff, as the enraged gypsy stared down the barrel of the executioner's pistol. The other men gathered around him, speaking in their own language, trying to persuade him to calm down.

The tension soon dissolved and the gypsy shook off the arms of his compatriots and stalked back to the camp the others following him.

The women stayed and looking the executioner in the eye said. "May you inherit his blood."

The executioner hurried back to his cart, her curses ringing in his ears.

On the occasion of her eighteenth birthday and coming of age, Arcadia Muller was thrown a huge party by her parents. Her parents, Hans and Ulrike, were by village standards well to do, farming some twenty acres of arable land and operating the only tavern in town. They had moved to the area nineteen years previously after Ulrike had surprisingly become pregnant. Her advanced years and lack of maternal instinct had the villagers foretelling an early death for her child, but the child had survived and today would enter adulthood.

Arcadia was an attractive girl, tall and slender with long flowing black hair. Her skin a dark brown, seldom seen in the southern mountains and possessing an infectious laugh which left an impression on all she met. She had lived a sheltered life in the village. Her parents had protected her from all they considered evil in the world, and consequently, by age eighteen she had become a very desirable and respected young woman.

Arcadia's outer beauty, however, disguised some serious emotional problems which had developed since her sixteenth year. To the distress of her parents, Arcadia had started hearing voices and at times talked of seeing wolves. That being said, Hans and Ulrike were overjoyed when a well-heeled young man named Gerd approached them, seeking to court Arcadia and her parents had agreed that when she reached adulthood they would permit a formal betrothal.

As the day wore on, the time when Hans would bring his daughter, by virtue of a small ceremony, into adulthood, got closer. The parents had erected a small marquee in the center of the village green. A large affair, with room for over a hundred guests underneath, it held a small wooden stage with a decorated throne where Arcadia was to be presented to the village as an adult at nightfall.

On the outskirts of the village was a small gypsy encampment. Shunned by the locals, the gypsies spent there lives scraping livings sharpening knives or selling herbal cures. The villagers, superstitious by nature, were also not averse to having their fortunes told by the gypsies and more for this reason than any other were the gypsies tolerated.

Some weeks before her eighteenth birthday, Arcadia had been asked by Gerd what she desired as a present. Without hesitating, she had replied that she would like to have her fortune told by the old gypsy women who lived in the encampment. Gerd was reluctant, knowing that her parents would never permit it. But after some pleading from Arcadia he agreed that on her eighteenth birthday during the late afternoon they would sneak away and she would have her wish.

By early evening the village and Arcadia's parents in a heightened state of enjoyment had turned their attentions away from the lady of the moment. Seeing their chance the two lovers slipped away and through a small meadow in the direction of the blazing campfires of the Gypsy settlement.

They entered the camp unchallenged; most of the gypsies were familiar with the locals trespassing and ignored them. The caravan they sought was dark and dreary. Standing outside the lovers knocked apprehensively on the door.

After some moments a crackly voice bade them come in and sit down. Climbing the two mud-caked steps at the rear, they pushed aside a red curtain and entered into a living area. The room was brightly decorated in red and gold, small glass baubles hung from the ceiling, and carpets hung on the walls hung.

Sitting cross-legged on the floor was an old wizened woman, her face wrinkled from years of sun exposure and wind burn; over her head she wore a shawl.

The lovers stood in the center of the room, and when the old lady motioned for them to sit, they remained standing. Local legend had it that to sit on a gypsy's carpet invited disease and bad luck. Arcadia squeezed Gerd's hand tightly; goose bumps appeared on her arm.

"Good evening, Arcadia Mandragora." said the old woman.

Arcadia looked quizzically at Gerd.

"I'm Arcadia Muller, Ma'am," she said.

"Arcadia Muller," repeated the Gypsy woman.

"Shut up you vile piece of garbage." said Gerd.

"As the master wishes," nodded the Gypsy

After an uncomfortable silence of a minute, Gerd started up again.

"She wants her fortune told," snapped Gerd, looking hard an Arcadia.

"Very well, young master," replied the woman. "Shall I tell past, present or future?"

The question was an odd onem and Gerd and Arcadia looked puzzled. Gerd thought a minute before saying, "The past is not a fortune, woman. Don't try your trickery here."

The old woman, ignoring Gerd, looked directly at Arcadia and asked, "Arcadia Mandragora, you pass into adulthood today. Would you leave your past behind?"

"You vile crone," said Gerd, raising his voice. "Just do as you're asked, and address her correctly."

"As the young master pleases," said the gypsy.

Cold as ice, the old women stared directly at Arcadia and spoke, "Goddess of the mandrakes you are born cursed and will die cursed."

Gerd strode across to the old gypsy, and raising his arm swiftly struck the gypsy across the face.

"You deplorable creature," he said, "I'll have you dragged and whipped for this."

The old woman held her face and spat at the feet of Gerd.

"Go, " she yelled. "My power is useless against her."

Dragging Arcadia by the hand, Gerd left the caravan, his lover in tears.

The voices and images that Arcadia had been experiencing the last two years were very loud that night. As the lovers passed through the forest on their return to the village green, Arcadia thought she saw a pack of wild wolves lurking behind some trees.

"Look," she screamed to Gerd. "Wolves."

"It's your imagination playing tricks with you," said Gerd grasping her hand more tightly.

"What did the gypsy mean?" she asked Gerd.

"I don't know," he answered. "It's all hocus pocus to me."

"The wolves are calling me, Gerd." said Arcadia.

Gerd had become somewhat used to these outbursts and ignored this one, pressing back toward the main village and Arcadia's birthday celebration.

"The wolves are trying to tell us something Gerd," continued Arcadia.

Gerd was beginning to worry. He was late in bringing Arcadia to her parent's house and she had started having her delusions again. Gerd did not want to be mean to his lover, but he thought a little discipline was needed.

"Arcadia, we must go back now," he said firmly.

Breaking from his grasp Arcadia ran off the forest track, into the dense undergrowth and out of sight. The light had worsened and Gerd cursed his luck at having to hunt for her in the dark.

Provocatively whistling and taunting Gerd, Arcadia stayed just out of his sight as he moved deeper into the forest.

"Arcadia," he yelled. "We must get back home now."

Further and further off the trail, Gerd searched and was just about to turn back when Arcadia, who had been sat waiting on a low branch, jumped on his back, wrapping her arms around his neck.

Gerd cursed as he fell to the ground, and Arcadia, with a strange strength, pinned her lover against the forest floor.

"Well, Gerd, I'm a woman at last." she said alluringly.

Gerd looked up at the full moon; he could make out lines and images in it, looking back up at Arcadia, her skirt pulled up over her knees Gerd gave in to his desires.

"I love you Arcadia. But we must go."

"I want to be on top," said Arcadia sensually.

The eager Gerd span around and wriggled under his woman. On top, she undid his trousers and started to arouse him. Gerd lay back and closed his eyes. His excitement evident in his screwed up eyes, Arcadia found herself imagining a gallows and a man with a wolf's head. About to ejaculate Gerd screamed at Arcadia and opened his eyes.

Arcadia, a smile on her face, plunged a dagger into his chest, as she imagined herself fighting off a wild wolf.

Arcadia got off Gerd, and sat on the grass next to his dead body. Carefully without missing a drop she transferred Gerd's harvested semen into a small leather bag, which she tucked next to her breast for warmth, then she walked back toward the forest trail.

Before she reached her house, she made a brief stop in the woods. Taking out the small leather bag from inside her dress, she carefully dropped some of the semen onto the ground next to a mandrake plant.

The cooks and other kitchen staff got up from their duties and left momentarily to join the celebration and Arcadia, resplendent in her evening gown, entered the kitchen. Speaking to her imaginary wolf friend, she poured the mandrake juice into the brandy mix. Stirring it quickly, she poured a glass. On her way out of the kitchen, she met the cook on his return.

The cook smirked at the site of the brandy glass and said, "Going to have a little tipple now you're a lady, Arcadia?"

Arcadia smiled and walked the glass upstairs to her mother, who drank it quickly.

"That's excellent," she commented. "Give my compliments to cook." After some thought she added. "Bring me another glass."

Arcadia nodded deferentially and went back down to the kitchen. By the time she returned her mother was dead.

The celebration was in full swing when one of the servants brought out a special cherry brandy for Hans, with the insistence that all present join the toast. The crowd waited for Hans to ascend the stage and when he did he filled his glass from the bowl next to Arcadia and raised it at the crowd, and his daughter now sat serenely on her throne in a toast.

Downing the first glass, he offered, as tradition dictated, a second glass and then a third.

By the time the third had been poured there was silence.

The crowd of people, so inebriated that they sensed little wrong, assumed Hans to have fallen over drunk on the stage and continued the celebration. It was not until the following morning that he was pronounced dead, a victim of mandrake poisoning.

Arcadia Muller met them same fate as her biological father. In Ravensberg that day, the crowd was very large, all there to see the tall, beautiful gypsy looking girl be hanged. After the town crier had read the sentence, the hangman, a jovial fellow from

Drumsdorf, fixed the noose to Arcadia's neck. Within a minute, she was dead.

As he was leaving the gallows site, a local woman accosted him and asked. "Did she have anything to say hangman?"

"Not really," replied the executioner. "Only, thank God I'm infertile."

The Legend of Baxter Mountain

Mountains are fascinating places. The silence they exude cannot be matched elsewhere, the array of fauna and wildlife abundant in its natural glory speaks of a bygone age before the advent of men, the solitude of a state a sometime longed by for each and every one of us.

Mountains also hold secrets, some dark and best not revealed, hidden behind rock faces and ledges. Mountains are home to strange people, a mixture of hermits and daredevils. When the secrets and people collide, the result is often stranger than fiction.

On Baxter Mountain, high above civilization, there lived a man named Obadiah Judson. Obadiah had sought the sanctuary of the highest altitudes, believing the solace that they afforded him would benefit his philosophical thought. Like many who are raised in an urban environment Obadiah had longed for privacy his whole life. He wanted the ability to stand and listen in peace without the constant interruptions of daily life. The right to breathe clean, unadulterated air, to live his life the way he chose.

He had, in later, started frequenting a small hunting cabin high in the Adirondacks. Accessible only eight months of the year, with the nearest neighbor five miles away on the other side of a sprawling valley, it was quiet and secluded. Obadiah had made the place home.

The cabin was small and compact, with two bedrooms, an eating area, kitchen and bathroom. It was sparsely furnished and built on a ledge which was surrounded by pine trees rendering it invisible to outsiders.

During the winter of 1938 Obadiah Judson received two visitors to the cabin. It had been a harsh winter, and in late January a particularly vicious storm dumped some twenty inches of snow on the mountain top, with more expected the following day. Obadiah braced himself for a long winter, hoping his supplies would last until spring.

On this particular evening, he had been laying another log on the small open fire he used for heat, when there was a knock at the cabin door. Assuming the knock to be a branch tapping somewhere on the cabin, Obadiah ignored it. However, once it was repeated, he walked over and opened the door.

Outside the wind was howling, blowing hard and fast as it often does on a mountain tops. When Obadiah opened the door, he was greeted with a wind gust so hard that he feared his humble fire may be blown out. In the snow outside stood a man, rucksack on his back and staff in his hand. The man appeared to be around thirty years of age with a full face beard, jaunty step and dark eyes. Obadiah, who had not spoken to anyone in some months, was lost for words. The tracks in the snow behind the traveler extended further up the mountain. Fool, thought Obadiah, to be out on a night like this.

"Come in," said Obadiah hurriedly, "But be quick. I don't want to lose all the heat from inside."

The traveler did not reply but made toward the entrance and followed Obadiah inside. Once inside, he took off his pack and laid it on the floor by the table, the snow falling easily off onto the cabin floor, where it melted. Obadiah motioned for the man to come sit by the fire.

Obadiah had but one chair. Rather than give it up, he indicated the traveler should sit on the rug. The traveler nodded his head in thanks and began to take off his boots.

From his chair by the fire, Obadiah studied his companion. The man was well built with large hands and a hooked nose. His face was worn and ruddy from the wind. Obadiah sensed that he was a man used to these harsh conditions.

Obadiah, who had just eaten, offered the man some bread. He smiled and took a piece, which he gobbled down hungrily, his stare never fixated on the fire. After the traveler had eaten several more slices of bread and drunk some wine, he stretched out on the rug, removed his socks and thanked Obadiah.

So long removed from civilization, Obadiah fancied conversation and, pouring himself and his new companion some more wine, he began.

"What brings you out on a night like this?" he asked, brushing his fringe away from his face.

The traveler looked at his host with an all knowing stare. The fire crackled and spat.

"I am searching for a lost traveler," he replied.

Obadiah smiled at the answer and for a moment longed to be alone again.

"You have picked a fine time to scale these peaks," Obadiah said.

"Are you from down there?" inquired Obadiah, lifting his head in the direction of the window.

"Yes, I suppose I am," answered his visitor his stare still fixed on the fire. "Although, not from that particular village."

Getting up from his chair, Obadiah walked over to a cupboard and took a pipe and tobacco jar out from it.

Returning to the fire-place, he filled the pipe and, poking a thin stick into the fire, waited for it to light. When it glowed red and hot lit his pipe.

The smoke from the pipe relaxed Obadiah some more, and, although his companion offered little conversation, he started to talk.

"These mountains are dangerous in such weather, my friend. You should not travel, and, if you must, at least have a companion."

"Are you my friend?" asked the visitor.

"It was a figure of speech." retorted Obadiah. "I have no friends, nor do I care to make any." He exhaled into the cabin as he spoke.

Silence descended again on the pair. Obadiah sucked on his pipe, and the traveler stared into the fire, a smile on his face, the heat further reddening his cheeks.

"For whom do you search this cold night?" asked Obadiah.

"For a friend of mine," replied the traveler.

"No one lives around here," said Obadiah. "The nearest house is many miles away. You must be lost."

"Really," answered the traveler, "I thought he had taken this route." Again he diverted his glance to Obadiah.

"Should you not have come with a search party?" asked Obadiah his teeth biting into the pipe's mouthpiece. "The village below has a rescue squad. I'm sure by early spring they will help you search."

He thought a moment and added, "How long has your friend been missing?"

The man on the rug stood up, and Obadiah again looked at his fine frame. The man must be six and a half feet tall. The traveler asked Obadiah if he could have more wine and Obadiah pointed to the pantry.

On his return, the traveler sat back down on the rug. The second glass of wine seemed to mellow him. He spoke to Obadiah.

"How long have you lived here?"

"Many years," said Obadiah. "I came here many years ago from faraway."

The stranger nodded.

Obadiah offered the man a bed for the night. The traveler, however, refused saying he must push on and look for his friend.

"Don't be stupid, man. There are nearly three feet of snow outside and the temperature is below zero. What could you accomplish out there tonight?" said Obadiah.

"I must find my friend," said the traveler.

"You will kill yourself out there," said Obadiah. "Just have some more wine and lie by the fire until morning. Your friend, if he has any sense, will be holed up in a cave somewhere."

The stranger accepted the offer of more wine, and he sat with Obadiah. The more wine they drank the more drowsy Obadiah became until he drifted into a hazy sleep. In his sleep Obadiah dreamed of his youth. On a small street in Horsham, he and his playmates chased another boy down a hill. In his dream Obadiah chased the boy, but it kept rolling down hill just out of his reach. He yelled at the ball, but could not catch it, eventually tripping on a protruding concrete slab and skinning his knee.

When Obadiah awoke the following morning, the stranger was gone. His initial reaction was to run outside and follow the man, but the morning was bitterly cold and Obadiah thought better of it. Muttering to himself, he made breakfast over the fire, still wondering where his visitor of the previous night had headed to. The storm would clear by mid-morning, he thought. Then maybe he would venture out to see what he could find.

Obadiah busied himself for the rest of the morning and, sure enough, by midday the storm's might had receded. Wrapping himself up warmly, he stepped outside. The snow was soft and fluffy and Obadiah sank in to his knees. The snow entered the top of his boots.

Cursing his luck before going back inside, Obadiah scanned the virgin snow quickly for sounds or sights of life. The traveler could not have gone far he thought. Even the best of outdoorsmen could not have gotten further than the edge of the ridge.

The cabin was situated about fifty yards from a stone ledge. The hard granite had formed centuries ago into a flat smooth surface in the shape of a heart, in summer the ledge afforded the looker an excellent view of the valley below and on a clear night the moon appeared so close that one could touch it. Once winter had set in however the ledge, ice covered underneath the snow pack became treacherous. Only someone familiar with the area knew its exact location.

Returning outside, Obadiah struggled some fifty yards or so in the snow before reaching the ledge. The overlook allowed him a sweeping view of the mountain slopes and the valley below. Obadiah pulled out his binoculars. In the distance, a figure appeared to be struggling down the mountainside, his stride cutting through the landscape like a giant butter knife. Looking more closely through his binoculars Obadiah spotted a crimson tinge along the traveler's path. He must be injured, thought Obadiah.

Cupping his hands to his mouth Obadiah yelled down at the lone figure.

"Wait. Come back. Are you hurt?"

Sound travels well in valleys during winter and Obadiah's words were clearly audible to the figure below, who turned around and gazed up the mountain, before continuing on his way with due haste.

What a fool, thought Obadiah, although he was relieved to see the man had made it down to the valley. Obadiah returned to his cabin.

The rest of the day Obadiah spent by the fireside warming himself and longing for the company of the previous night. At six it was dark outside again, and Obadiah prepared to turn in early. Sitting by his fire he heard another knock on the door.

Opening the door to the clear winter night, Obadiah was shocked to see a different visitor at his door. This fellow was shorter and thinner. His eyes were narrow, giving him a dishonest look; he was poorly clothed for the winter and shivered uncontrollably.

Beckoning him inside, Obadiah offered the stranger food and warmth as he had done his visitor of the previous night. The two of them conversed at ease by the fire.

"What brings you up here this cold night?" asked Obadiah

The stranger seemed reluctant to reply, his eyes staring around furtively as if expecting something to happen. The trees outside creaked in the frozen wind, their branches rubbing eerily against the side of the cabin.

The stranger seemed reluctant to talk and Obadiah found it hard to elicit any conversation from him. Offering him more wine in the hope of loosening his tongue, Obadiah found himself becoming tipsy as he matched the stranger drink for drink. Lighting his pipe as he had done the previous night, he blurted out,

"You're not very talkative at all. Even the fellow from last night had more to say."

The comment aroused the silent stranger. His eyes narrowed and looked fearful. He spoke quickly, his speech jerking in a stammer.

"You saw him. What did he want? Where did he go?"

"What a lot of questions," replied Obadiah. "I'm afraid I don't know the answers to them." He stoked the fire with a poker.

"But did he ask for me?" asked the stranger.

"I don't know who you are," answered Obadiah. Then he continued, "He did say he was looking for someone."

The stranger asked what Obadiah's visitor from the previous night had looked like.

"Well, he was a big fellow," said Obadiah. "A trifle shy, didn't say much, like you. He had a full beard with large dark eyes. He looked like a friendly type to me."

The stranger stood up and moved nearer to Obadiah saying, "Well he's no good. Don't you let him in again, you hear? He's dangerous."

Obadiah, a little taken aback by the outburst and needled by the stranger's tone, retorted quickly, "I choose whom I receive in my house." Helping himself to more wine, he added, "He seemed like a decent fellow to me."

"You don't know him," started the stranger. "He kills people."

Obadiah felt that the tone of the conversation was going downhill. His head muzzy from wine, his false courage at its height, he took a different tone.

"I don't like this," he said. "If you wish to stay, stay. Or get out. Either way, this conversation is over."

Surprised by his own courage, Obadiah stood threateningly over the thin stranger.

To his surprise, the stranger quickly dressed, leaving his mittens behind, and left, closing the door behind him. Obadiah started to get up to stop him, but for the second night began to feel drowsy as the wine muddled his head. He fell asleep in his chair and dreamt of chasing the same young man downhill. The boy ever increasing in speed ran beyond the reach of Obadiah and into the path of an on coming car. The car swerved to avoid the boy and plunged headlong into a gorge which ran alongside the road.

Obadiah awoke and ventured outside again. The snow was firmer from a night in the frozen air and he walked easily to the ledge and once again scanned the slopes. Obadiah at first did not see the body at his feet. The skinny visitor of the previous night laid dead, frozen solid, his eyes looking imploringly up at the sky, his hands gnarled and curled as if holding an imaginary object.

Obadiah looked at the frozen figure his face trapped in time. Should he bury the unfortunate stranger? Feeling it was his obligation to at least cover the stranger, he searched the landscape for fallen branches. Finding some, he laid them over the stranger and then attempted to bury him with loose snow.

That night it snowed some more, and during the next month several feet fell. Spring came late and when it did the melt and heavy rains washed the debris down the mountainside and into the river below. So serious was the flooding that the village below was under a flash flood warning at least three times during April.

Consequently it was late May before Obadiah ventured down the mountain into town for some provisions. Even at this late stage the hike down was hard.

Stopping at the local police station, Obadiah reported the death of his second visitor. The policeman on desk duty viewed the report with some suspicion and asked Obadiah to take a seat and wait while he filed a report. Returning to the waiting room he asked Obadiah to describe the man.

As best as he could Obadiah described the small weasel-like man who had visited him that night and the story he had recounted about the killer out to get him.

"You have to remember, Officer, this all took place some months ago and I only saw him briefly," said Obadiah.

After taking the report down, the police officer showed Obadiah a photograph of a dead figure lying in the snow by the police station. His throat appeared to have been cut, the eyes wider than Obadiah remembered.

"This wasn't the man was it sir?"

"That," said Obadiah with a straight face, "was my first visitor. He stopped in the night before."

The policeman nodded in apparent comprehension.

"This guy came here in late February," he said. "Couldn't speak poor fellow. He must have lost a gallon of blood. He kept pointing up the mountain. His throat has been cut from ear to ear."

"Must have been that other thin fellow," surmised Obadiah. "I didn't like the look of him at all."

The officer nodded.

As he was leaving the sergeant on duty came into the waiting room to join his junior colleague. Looking oddly at Obadiah he asked.

"Is everything okay up there on the mountain, Sir?"

"Yes," said Obadiah.

"Would you like an escort sir? It's very remote up there."

"No, thank you." replied Obadiah. "I know the way."

"Did you leave an address sir?" asked the Sergeant. "In case we need to contact you."

"No," replied Obadiah. "I receive my correspondence in the village."

"And your name, Sir?" asked the sergeant.

"Galvin," replied Obadiah. "Thomas Galvin."

Before the sergeant could make further inquiries, Obadiah left the police station. The junior officer asked his sergeant if he should pursue him. The sergeant shook his head.

"This is the second year we've had people missing on Baxter Mountain. Those hunting cabins are so remote. Who knows what goes on up there?"

By the time the sergeant had finished, Obadiah Judson was already on his way back up the mountain.

When he arrived back at the cabin, Obadiah fell asleep. In his dream he caught the young man he had been chasing. By the following autumn he started placing the signs along the ski trail which ran two hundred feet above the cabin as he did before every winter season. He took special care with those that pointed the way to shelter and food for any traveler caught on the mountain during a winter storm.

Pierre, Marie and the Christmas Tree

Marie was late decorating her apartment for Christmas. In the years since she had emigrated from Poland, Marie had never been as tardy as she was that year. Her mother had often warned her of forsaking her private enjoyment for work, and for the most part her stubborn daughter had listened. This year, however, those words had been lost to the heavy volume of work at the laboratory. Both Marie and her husband Pierre had left it until Christmas Eve to decorate their apartment.

To make matters worse their four-year-old child Mischa was at the age where she could first comprehend and appreciate holidays, this had made Marie feel a little guilty.

As she took the tram home from the university Marie began to feel even guiltier. She wondered whether it was the curse of the brilliant never to enjoy the holidays. True it had been a struggle for Marie. Being a women in a male dominated world, she had been forced to work a little harder and stay a little longer at most levels of her education, but now she had some security and it had been augmented by her marriage to Pierre.

During the tram ride, Marie watched the gaily-clad Parisians going about their festive business. It stirred a longing in her heart one she had not known since childhood.

Seeing herself two stops away from her street, she pulled the cord. The tram soon stopped and Marie alighted watching her steps carefully as she descended. Crossing to the pavement, Marie gazed around. She realized it had been many months since she had even been shopping, leaving such chores to her domestic help.

Making her way along the pavement, she occasionally stopped to look in store windows, admiring the brightly decorated displays. It was cold outside, so Marie stuck her hands in her overcoat pocket. At the bottom of her left pocket, she felt something. She thought, then laughed. Pierre had given her several pieces of isolated radium the previous day and Marie, liking the strange glow they had emitted, absent-mindedly placed them in her pocket. The rocks provided a little warmth for Marie's hands as she traversed the street.

A new fad in Paris that year had been the use of fir trees as a Christmas symbol. Marie looked at a store front which was filled with evergreens and decided she must have one. In and out of several stores, she went looking for the best bargain, eventually settling on a three-foot model with modest branches. She arranged to have it delivered later that day to her apartment. On her way out of the store, Marie stopped to look at the glass baubles and candles that the shopkeeper had decorated his tree with. Impressed, she inquired as to the cost, but alas the shopkeeper informed her he had sold out sometime earlier that day.

After doing some other sundry shopping, Marie decided to walk home. The general merriment of Paris at Christmas is second to none and the normally reserved Pole's eyes lit up. Turning onto her street, she noticed it was getting dark. The gaslights on her street were lit; emanating pale haloes further enraptured Marie.

Entering her apartment Marie found Pierre already home. He had been lecturing at the Sorbonne that morning at had come home early to spend time with his lady folk. The cook had prepared alight snack, and the family sat down to eat.

Marie was nervous about telling Pierre about the Christmas tree. She broached the subject carefully knowing her husband did not care for flamboyance. But she was pleasantly surprised by his response. He admitted that he thought of buying a tree but decided against it because he did not know how Marie would react.

After they had eaten, Pierre and Marie cleared an area in the corner of the living room. Marie found a large sheet which she spread over the area to catch the pine-needles. Their daughter was much enthused by the activity, crawling around on the sheet and grinning at her parents.

Sometime later, the delivery man arrived with the tree. After bringing it into the apartment, he helped Marie and Pierre place it into a giant earth-filled pot from their balcony. It took several tries to get the fir tree as straight as Marie liked. After being paid, the man wished both of them merry Christmas and left.

I was now totally dark, and Marie and Pierre lit candles. For a while they stood hand in hand and admired their tree. Mischa rolled on the floor giggling, the candlelight catching her every expression.

Then with an artistic bent she had not shown since childhood, Marie announced they would decorate the tree. Having no decorations, the pair started to improvise. Any shiny material they could find, they attached to the branches. Pierre added some tinsel he had found in the stairwell of their apartment building. After they had finished, they once again stood back and admired the tree.

It was looking at little strange though. The two scientists moved closer holding their candles.

"It needs light," said Pierre.

Marie said that she was not comfortable putting candles on her tree.

"It may catch fire," she said.

"It just looks a little dour like that," said Pierre.

Marie knew this was true and began thinking quickly. Going into the kitchen she asked the cook for several empty jars. The cook spent sometime looking in the pantry and returned with three old glass jars about six inches in length.

Marie walked over to her coat and took out the rocks from her pocket. She unscrewed the jar lids, threw several rocks into each and the refastened the tops.

Seeing what was happening, Pierre produced some small pieces of string, made loops, and attached them firmly to the necks of the jars. Together, the two walked over to the Christmas tree and hung the jars on branches.

The light emitted from the jars was beautiful pale green. It lit up the room and gave it spiritual feel.

Their daughter giggled and laughed herself to sleep that night whilst her mother and father stared bewitched at the tree.

In a magazine interview at the Sorbonne some years later, Marie was asked to what extent she thought her discoveries had benefitted mankind. She answered falteringly that she was sure that Radium had sparked considerable research in certain areas. Then as an adage, she quipped, that if put in glass jars, it makes a great Christmas decoration.

Good Friday

The strong April sun hung heavily on the governor's mansion that Friday morning and the bright white building stood firmly within its gaze, reflecting the approaches, shadowing the rear.

In the governor's office, all was quiet, not even the scratch of a pen was audible as the man who held the lives of others in the palm of his hand reflected on his day.

Executions had been rare in Florida for the last decade, and Governor Pat Romano was glad. For truth be told, although his electorate supported the death penalty, he himself had grave reservations.

This particular Friday, however, four death warrants awaited him on his desk.

Romano glanced over the warrants briefly and walked over to a large armchair in the corner of the room. Sitting down legs crossed he contemplated the situation, running his hands slowly over the soft leather arms. Since his tenure began three years ago, Romano had skillfully delegated this kind of problem to his lieutenant governor, who had managed to negotiate stays and commutations. So, to date Romano had yet to sign a death warrant.

On this occasion, however, the Lieutenant Governor had been unable to procure the normal commutations. Declining to confirm the death sentences himself, the Lieutenant Governor had bounced them back up to Romano.

The Governor's mansion can be a very lonely place at such times. In the days prior, Romano had sought the best council for his decision.

The people he had consulted, his wife, his cleric and his former commanding officer, all had the same observation: The death penalty was barbaric and as applied, it officially sanctioned the taking of a life, which was contrary to all moral and ethical standards applied elsewhere in the world.

Romano knew that the majority of the population supported the death penalty, and if he failed to act accordingly, his chances of re-election were thin.

Sitting in his chair that Friday Romano began for the first time in his life to contemplate the moral implications of signing the warrants.

At fifty, Governor Romano was a successful man, having fully lived the American dream. He had been born into a working class family in New Jersey. His father a soldier, his mother a homemaker and amateur fortune teller.

By eighteen he had enlisted in the army and seen active duty in Vietnam. Returning home a local hero he had skillfully used his new found fame in business, becoming, by age forty, a wealthy man.

That year at a Christmas party someone had suggested that Romano run for public office. Thus began a successful political career, culminating ten years later in his landslide victory in the Florida governor's race.

The governor, now extremely popular, had been spoken of as a candidate for higher office. Now his every move was under scrutiny, there was no room for errors.

Romano knew what it was like to kill someone. As a young soldier during the jungle wars of sixty-five his unit had attacked a Vietcong tunnel complex. Flamethrowers had flushed most of the enemy out and Roman and several other privates had met them with machine gun fire at the tunnel's entrance.

Slaughtering defenseless men is a harrowing experience and Romano had not enjoyed it. The memory of that day had been selectively stored in his subconscious.

The governor winced as he thought of the moment. At the time he had promised himself that he would have no one else's blood on his hands. That appeared about to change today.

Governor Romano's time had run out. The men were scheduled to die by lethal injection that Friday evening. All Romano's delaying options had been exhausted. The death warrants lay on his desk and he had eight hours to sign them.

Sitting in his comfortable chair a flash of brilliance ran through the Governor's mind. Why not pardon someone that Friday, in honor of Easter. The more the idea took root the more sensible it appeared to the Governor. Maybe, he opined, he could pardon them all.

Romano walked back to his desk and buzzed in his secretary.

Without looking up from the death warrants he asked his secretary to contact the attorney general immediately.

Death warrants are odd affairs and as he stared at the documents on his desk Romano mused he had seen, or dreamt such a situation before.

The state's attorney general James Pope was shown into the Governor's office an hour later. As was the case with the secretary he found Romano sitting completely still at his desk staring blankly at the death warrants.

The attorney general coughed.

The Governor looked up slowly as if in a trance, his eyes wide and searching.

"Ah, James," he said.

"You sent for me sir?" said James.

"Yeah," began the governor slowly. "It's this death warrant business. I'm feeling a little, let's say uncomfortable." Romano sounded out the last word slowly, syllable by syllable.

"How can I help you sir?" asked James, still standing up in front of the governor's desk.

Romano toyed with the pen in his hand, appearing deep in thought.

"Is there anyway out of this unfortunate business?" he asked.

"Please sit down." he added.

"The death warrants?" asked James.

"What other pressing business would I have summoned you here immediately for?" said Romano sarcastically.

"Maybe some legislative matter?" queried James.

Governor Romano suddenly became aware that he may be the only person in the administration who was somewhat concerned that four people were about to be put to death.

"Where do we stand, legally?" he asked.

"As regards?" replied James.

"As regards clemency, man," said Romano raising his voice and becoming more direct in his tone.

"Clemency?" asked the bemused attorney general.

"Yes." snapped Romano.

The attorney general was well-versed in the legal aspects of the cases. He crossed his legs and did his best to outline the governor's options.

"Two of these individuals were convicted by Federal courts sir. So they do not technically fall under your jurisdiction. The other two cases however, those of Barbara and Goodman, are local convictions. Did you send them back down to the appellate court?"

The governor nodded.

"The law as it reads provides you with the right to grant clemency, but the quirk is you can only pardon one man. The law is quite clear two simultaneous applications for clemency cannot be approved. It's to prevent a catch 22 situation."

"So," said Roman. "in a nutshell, I get to pardon one of these guys."

"In a nutshell, yes." replied James.

Romano was silent.

"If I may suggest something sir," began James. "You should review the files on the two men and make a speedy decision."

Romano nodded.

The two men exchanged a few comments and wished each other a happy Easter.

Once his attorney general had left, Governor Romano continued to contemplate his dilemma.

The four men who were to die that Friday evening had been convicted of a variety of crimes. Two had killed federal marshals in the course of a robbery and therefore were not the responsibility of the state. The other two, however, had committed crimes which fell under the governor's jurisdiction and it was from these two that Romano had to choose one befitting of clemency.

Romano had little interest in the smaller workings of state government. On that morning, he was obliged to review the men's files and decide on whom to grant clemency.

Buzzing for his secretary, the governor gazed out of the huge French windows to his right. It looked like a fine morning, spring was finally in the air and the Governor opened the French doors to let in the breeze. Then sitting behind his desk, he picked up the two files.

The first man, Lorenzo Barbara, was a Maltese immigrant who was a career criminal. Most of his youth had been spent in reformatory schools, and he appeared to have risen the ranks of crime steadily over the last twenty years, culminating in a violent armed robbery one night five years ago, where he had killed a security guard.

The second man, Simon Goodman, had been prosecuted under the states new anti-terrorism laws. He was, it appeared, a rabble rouser. His history was that of a subversive. He opposed taxation and government control. This had found him quite a public following. He had, on the evidence of several high ranking officials, been accused of making terroristic threats and seeking to overthrow the government. The transcript of his trial was in the Governor's folder, but, Romano whose mind was elsewhere did not review it. Instead, he buzzed his secretary.

"Yes sir," answered the woman, entering the room and closing the door behind her.

Romano motioned that she should sit and he dictated a short letter to the prison warden indicating that he would like to visit both of the condemned men that morning.

Then asking her to leave Romano strolled leisurely out into the garden admiring the excellent fauna already half in bloom.

So lost was Romano in his thoughts that morning that he did not notice his returning secretary who had entered the garden looking for him.

"Yes," he asked.

The secretary went on to tell him that due a manpower shortage the Governor's visit to the prison could not be arranged. The prison warden was also once again requesting the signed death warrants for Goodman and Barbara.

It was then that Romano did something completely unconventional.

"Well, bring the men here." he said. "I'll interview them right here in the garden."

The secretary looked shocked.

"Sir....." she stammered.

But Roman was a forceful and convincing man.

"Do as I say. That's an executive order. I expect them here by noon."

The secretary knew better than to argue and disappeared, heels clicking back into the mansion.

Romano continued to walk the gardens well-laid out paths. Toward the end of the rose garden was a small rectangular pond. The area around it decorated in a classical style. Several large colonnades on either side of the pond led to a small replica of a Greek temple at the north end. Stopping to look in a small pond the Governor noticed a large stone chair beyond the pond, with three steps leading up to it, shaded by the temple roof.

Romano walked up the steps, dusted some of the moss off the seat with his hand, and he sat down. The chair was large and in design resembled a throne. The back and arms intricately decorated with classical figures, the legs in the shape of a clasping lion's paw.

The security detail which entered the garden that Friday had some difficulty locating the governor at first. Several men searched the garden area and were surprised to find the governor sitting in a stone chair. His secretary sat some five feet to his on an ornamental bench.

"Sir," started a security man. "the condemned men are here."

Looking down from his stone throne, Governor Romano, with a rolled up file in hand, boomed down at the officer.

"Okay. Bring me Barbara first."

The officer disappeared and returned five minutes later, somewhat shaken.

"Barbara is having a fit of madness," he said. "It might not be wise, Sir."

Holding up his hand in an ever regal manner Romano cut the officer short.

"I wish to see this man," he said, his throne giving new authority.

Four guards brought the struggling Barbara to stand before the governor. The prisoner spat on the mosaic square and launched into a tirade about the prison system, coloring his diatribe with any obscenity he could think of.

After five minutes, he appeared out of both breath and words, so Romano, sitting, addressed the virulent figure.

"Mr. Barbara, I have deigned to spare someone's life today. Judging by what you say, you feel aggrieved. Please in your own words tell me why I should grant you clemency."

Barbara, although heavily shackled, lunged forward toward the steps leading up to where Romano was sat. He stumbled and fell after several tries to walk in Romano's direction, his large frame crashing onto the concrete.

"Please try and contain your emotions, Mr. Barbara," said the Governor.

Once again Barbara launched into a spasm of verbal abuse, at the end of which the Governor motioned for the guards to take him away.

"Lunatic," he said to his secretary. "Now what about some lunch?"

The secretary disappeared back into the direction of the mansion, leaving Romano alone for some minutes. After dusting his jacket, he glanced over the charge sheet in his hand.

The secretary returned with a kitchen employee. Lunch was to be cold, a bowl of fruit, some bread and various cuts of meat. All this topped with the governor's favorite wine, a deep full-bodied red.

Setting a small table down next to the Governor, the staff member placed the tray with the food on it and withdrew. Romano's secretary sat herself back down on the bench and awaited his instruction.

After taking a few mouthfuls of food the Governor, relaxed, glass in hand, and asked his secretary a question.

"This next fellow, Goodman, is this all they have on him?" he asked, waving the charge sheet now rolled up in his fist.

The secretary nodded.

The second man brought before the Governor that morning was a bedraggled figure. Small in stature he was some weeks unshaven, his long hair felt untidily on the prison uniform he was wearing. Flanked by two burly guards and the prison warden he shuffled toward the small concrete square before the governor's stone chair, eyes squinting in the bright April sun.

The governor, who had been dreaming of his impending vacation, glanced at the wretched figure now standing chained before him.

Taking stock of the man, Romano guessed him to be about thirty years of age. Behind his mass of hair were keen brown eyes and sharp Semitic features.

Eating his lunch, the governor poured himself another glass of red wine. The wine was bitter and Romano coughed.

Addressing the prisoner, he began.

"Sedition is an unfortunate charge, Goodman. Some years ago it would have carried a short prison sentence, but times change. You are due on the gurney tonight. Please tell me why I should show you mercy."

Goodman shuffled uncomfortably, his shackled wrists already chaffed and sore.

"Well," said Romano a little louder. "Are you going to speak?"

The prisoner stared back at Romano.

Romano was beginning to lose patience with the man.

"Listen Goodman, less than ten hours from now you are scheduled to die by lethal injection. If you have anything to say in your defense or have some good reason why I should grant you clemency speak up now."

Goodman stood silently in front of the seated governor.

"Where's the evidence file dealing with this man?" demanded the governor.

His secretary quickly got up and handed him Goodman's appellant file.

Romano was a quick reader and the file was short. The prisoner it appeared had been subject to a small closed door trial as the new terrorist laws allowed for. The three judges had found Goodman guilty as charged. Goodman had chosen to defend himself and, according to the transcript, said very little at his trial.

Leaning back on his stone throne, Romano spoke quietly to his prisoner.

"It says here that you entered the capital from the east, where you were met by a rabble or criminal element. Is this true?"

"No," replied the prisoner.

"So all these people are lying?"

"I do not know," replied the bewildered prisoner. "I have been resident here for several years. I did enter the city that day, but it was by train."

"Who are this rabble who met you?" asked Romano

"I came alone." replied the prisoner quietly.

"Are you a vagrant?" asked the Governor.

"I don't consider myself a vagrant. I travel a lot. But I don't sleep on the street."

Romano frowned.

"You were arrested in the city park after dark?" he asked.

"Sir, it is not a crime to be in the city park after dark. It is a peaceful place. I wanted to think."

"It says here you were with mob of people."

"No governor. I had only one man with me, a friend of mine."

"Who?" asked the puzzled Governor.

"An old friend named Jules, Governor."

Romano, his patience wearing thin, was short with Goodman.

"Goodman. In my profession I meet all manner of unsavory sorts. From thieves to cheats to liars. You are a liar."

Goodman did not reply, still staring at Romano who was beginning to feel uncomfortable with his gaze.

"Governor." began Goodman nervously. "Do you believe in the truth?"

Romano's gaze fell on the wretched figure, and, however he tried to prevent himself from answering, he could not help himself.

"I beg your pardon." said Romano, astonished at the man's audacity.

"Do you believe in the truth?" repeated the prisoner.

"Of course I believe in the truth. I live by the truth. My life is based upon the truth."

"Then why do you believe other people when they lie?"

For the first time during the interview, Romano was beginning to feel uncomfortable. He changed the subject quickly.

"It says here you entered the state house finance committee meeting and started a riot."

"It was not a riot, governor, for I was the only person there."

Romano picked up the file and read.

"It says you and a mob of criminals entered the state house. Here in black and white."

"Governor, do you believe that a mob could pass through state house security?" asked Goodman smiling.

The governor coughed and asked for a glass of water. Then, gazing eastward avoiding the prisoner's stare, he asked. "So what happened then?"

Goodman, his legs still rattling the chains, explained.

"I merely went to the reception desk at the state house and asked to meet the finance committee, as I believe is my right."

"Criminals are not permitted in the state house," answered Romano coldly.

"I had not been convicted of any crime," answered Goodman.

Reading the file, Romano found that prior to his arrest there was no criminal history on the prisoner.

"Maybe it was your appearance?"

"I was clean shaven that day."

"Maybe you got over emotional, started to shout, made threats," suggested Romano.

"No, Sir, I was quite calm."

Standing up, the governor pulled his jacket closed and buttoned it.

"Are you trying to suggest that all this is fabricated?" he said sternly, waving the evidence file in his hand.

"I don't know." said the prisoner. "I've never read it."

Roman walked to the temple's limit; something was bothering the governor about this man.

"I am obliged," started Romano, "to take this evidence as the truth, but if you would care to explain the events to me in your own words, I'll listen."

"Really, Sir." cut in the warden. "We don't have time. The man has already been tried and condemned."

"Shut up," shouted Romano. "This man is to die in six hours. Will you deny him?"

Shocked and hurt, the warden, at the bidding of the secretary, sat back down.

"Governor," began Goodman slowly. "I went to the statehouse to attempt to speak to a member of the finance committee."

"Why?" asked Romano.

"Because they are withholding money, money that could be used to feed the poor, they have been debating a grant for impoverished families for a year now. "

"So." asked Romano

"Governor, they managed to pass the tax cut packages in an hour and attached a large pay raise for themselves. But the poverty relief bill has been stuck in committee for a year," said Goodman.

"Things take time in government, you know," said Romano unconvincingly.

"Governor, how many people will die in the next year? How much blood do you have on your hands?"

Governor Romano's face reddened in anger and glaring down at the prisoner, he yelled,

"Shut it, you miserable man. I invited you here to appeal for mercy and you insult me as if I'm the criminal. Have you no respect? Take this man away," he yelled.

The guards and a relieved warden duly obliged and Goodman shuffled away.

Sitting on his chair Romano held his head in hands. Well that's over he thought.

After sitting for some time Romano opened his eyes and addressed his secretary.

"Go and bring that wretched man back here now," he barked hastily.

"I think they've left," replied the secretary.

"Then run after them, for the love of God," shouted the increasingly agitated governor. "Run." he added.

The secretary stood up and started running after the recently departed group. In doing so, she dropped the papers she had been holding. Ever the organized man, Romano walked down from the temple and picked the papers up.

Shuffling them into some sort of order Romano glanced at the top paper. It was a detailed commentary on Goodman's arrest. Then Governor walked back up to the temple and sat down. Eyes barely blinking he began to read.......

Simon Goodman, aged thirty, was arrested on the orders of the House speaker Kampf. Kampf's decision was based upon evidence provided by a friend of Goodman's named Jules Gelt. For this service, the man had been paid thirty thousand dollars, an amount which had been immediately approved by the finance committee.

The charge of sedition was a complicated one. Because of the events of the last ten years sedition trials were held in private. The accused was granted the right to a lawyer, but the trial information was a closely guarded secret. The defendant's lawyer was not granted the right to review the evidence against his client prior to the trial. This would breach the official restrictions imposed by the now all powerful Patriot act.

The accused was tried before a panel of three judges who determined the verdict. As in the regular court system, there were only two possible verdicts guilt or acquittal.

Acquittal was rare and guilty verdicts carried severe punishment, anywhere from thirty years to the death sentence.

Once sentenced the accused had the right of appeal, the appeal was brought before a similar three judge panel which met behind close doors. When they had issued their findings the accused had but one recourse, a direct appeal to the governor.

Few such cases occurred in Florida and so there was no historical precedent for the governor to refer to for guidance.

One of the larger problems was that the Patriot act severely restricted the sharing of sensitive information, as such much of the court transcript was blacked out.

Staring in disbelief at the half blacked-out page, Romano was interrupted by the returning secretary saying that she had been unable to stop the convoy from leaving the mansion.

"Dammit," said the Governor under his breath.

"Get me the speaker of the house," barked Romano.

"The house is in recess until after Easter," answered the secretary.

"I don't give a damn if the man is on the moon. Get him here now or no warrants are going to be signed."

The secretary knew better than to argue with her employer and once again left the Governor sitting on his stone chair.

Kampf, the speaker of the state house of representatives was a tall, thin man with pursed lips. Entering the garden that Friday afternoon, it was sometime before he could locate Governor

Romano, who had moved into a rose plantation, where he stood fingering a blooming plant.

After exchanging a few niceties, the Governor outlined his position. He had decided that in celebration of the upcoming Easter holiday, he was to grant clemency to one of the four condemned men. The first two had committed federal crimes and so were the business of the federal authorities. So that left him with Barbara and Goodman. Did the speaker care to propose a candidate?

Kampf, answered,

"It is a magnanimous gesture, Sir. The house requests you commute the sentence of Barbara."

Romano was little surprised, but he hid it skillfully. Saying that he did not wish to interfere in the workings of the state government, but he believed an error was being made. He asked Kampf to reconsider.

Kampf replied that the question had been discussed at length with the other ranking members of the house and the decision was to ask for clemency for Barbara.

The governor stared out at his beautiful surroundings. The smell of spring that had caught him by surprise earlier that morning was now in full evidence. The day had become warm as well. This being the case, the governor suggested that the two retire to the balcony of the mansion to seek some relief.

Much of the discussion between the garden and the balcony was on non-essential state matters, but once seated on the balcony the conversation again reverted to the clemency issue.

"This man, Goodman," began the governor. "I'm not sure I totally follow what his crime was."

"Sedition," replied Kampf.

"Yes. But what actually did he do?" pressed the governor.

Kampf, without being rude, tried to inveigh to Romano that the crime was a legal matter with which he should not concern himself. The evidence had been damning.

"But I am concerned," continued the governor. "In my office is a death warrant which has to be signed. I need to know why."

Kampf had been expecting the question and he had a quick answer.

"The man is a terrorist. He incited a riot against the state. He spreads a doctrine of civil disobedience."

"But his crime," persisted Romano.

"The evidence is in his file. He was going to blow up the state offices."

"The file is nearly totally blacked out," commented Romano.

"That's a security matter, Sir. I can assure you there was plenty of evidence," said Kampf.

"Based upon the evidence of this one other man?" asked the Governor.

"There were others," answered Kampf his eyes shifting.

"Where are they?" asked the Governor.

"Who knows," said Kampf shrugging his shoulders.

"I should like to interview them," said the Governor. "I think I'll stay this man's execution until I can review the evidence."

Kampf's face darkened. Taking a drink of his wine he replied carefully.

"Sir, the man has exhausted all legal remedies. He has no right of appeal. The evidence has been examined by the finest legal minds. He is guilty of sedition and must die this evening."

"Unless I commute his sentence." added Romano.

"That would be unwise." said Kampf deliberately. "In the statehouse he is considered a threat."

Romano drank his wine and stood up. Walking to the edge of the balcony he placed both hands on the rail and looked down into the garden.

"Tell me, Kampf," he said without turning round. "Does your conscience bother you?"

"No," snapped Kampf. "I sleep very well."

Governor Romano was never a man to act on impulse, but that day was different. Spinning around quickly, he trained his gaze upon the speaker.

"Kampf. Do you take me for a fool?"

The speaker did not reply.

"Really Kampf, look at this." he said shaking the file at Kampf.

"This is your evidence, the word of glad-mouthers, gossipers and petty criminals. How did this get this far? It is nonsense. This man isn't a danger. At best he's a deluded."

Kampf said nothing.

"Please tell me again. Who would you have me spare? Barbara, who killed a man and has probably killed several others during his criminal career. Or this other man, who's only crime is asking that you tell the truth. Deal with pressing situations, poverty and social issues. You would take a man's life for that? Come on."

Kampf was not used to being talked to so directly. He chose his words carefully.

"Governor, there is no law pertaining to these social issues. The state has a responsibility. Remember those attacks ten years ago. They threatened our way of life. Would you have this man rouse another bunch of terrorists, this time homegrown? Take responsibility for your actions, Governor. He is a man who threatens us all."

Governor Romano disliked Kampf, but knew he must be careful in his dealings with the man. Trying a different tack he asked.

"The chief witness against this lunatic was this man Jules Gelt."

"Yes," replied Kampf.

"For which you paid him the handsome sum of thirty thousand dollars."

"That was the deal," replied Kampf. "Sir, it's sometimes difficult to recognize one of these people from the other. We needed a positive identification. This other fellow could provide it."

"For thirty thousand dollars, I'd provide it," yelled the governor.

Kampf collected himself and once again replied that it was a positive identification.

"What happened to this other fellow?" asked the governor.

Kampf shrugged his shoulders.

"So if anyone were to want to contact this Gelt, where would he find him?" asked Romano.

Kampf again remained defiantly silent.

The governor walked over to the table where he poured himself another glass of wine. Drinking a large gulp his eyes glistened.

"Now listen, Speaker. Do you think I don't understand this nonsense?"

"Not completely," replied Kampf. "And I don't believe it's nonsense."

The tone and articulation was too much for the governor. His tongue was now loosened by several glasses of wine.

Pointing his finger at the speaker and thrusting his face in his, he shouted.

"This is it Kampf. One time only. I'm done with this. You think I don't understand what you and your compatriots are doing over there?" He swung his hand in the direction of the state house.

"From now on I'm watching you. You wretched people will have no peace. I'll see to that. I'll order every transcript of every session you've ever had and I'll read them. No black outs. Every secret court that's convened, I'll be there. You people are not getting away with executing someone whose only crime was to tell the truth, about you and you miserable scheming. Do you hear me speaker?"

"Careful governor." said Kampf. "These are laws. We live by the law. Do not think beyond your station Governor. Supporting seditious behavior is also a crime."

"Do you threaten me speaker?" barked Romano in reply. "Do you think me scared? Mark my words. No peace for you people from today on. I intend to turn the statehouse on its head."

Kampf pursed his lips further and remained silent.

"Well," began Romano changing his tone. "This has all been very pleasant, but the world continues to turn. You shall have the death warrants within an hour."

Kampf stood up and made a few comments about the weather and left as silently as he had come.

Tired from the days events the Governor ambled back into his office. Yawning he loosened his tie and sat down on the sofa. The Governor was confused. This man Goodman did not appear to be the violent threat that everyone claimed he was. He was sure he had seen or heard of the man someplace before, but he could not bring it to mind.

Stretching out on the sofa, Romano closed his eyes momentarily.

Romano was a vivid dreamer and that afternoon was no different.

In the early part of his dream the Governor was sitting in a pastoral scene. A clear green meadow bordered on one side by a small river. All was calm and the Governor was sat at a bright silver table.

A simple meal had been prepared for him at the table, a loaf of bread and a large overflowing goblet of red wine. Looking up from his table Romano saw the pasture was full of lambs. One of the lambs, white and fluffy, trotted over to the Governor, who in a moment of humility petted it as he did he knocked over the goblet, spilling the blood red wine onto the table cloth and lamb, where it soaked in quickly, leaving a dark stain on the lamb.

Romano rose from the silver table and chased the wine-stained lamb across the pastures.

As he dreamt, the scene changed. Gone were the luscious pastures and spring lambs, replaced by a narrow canyon lined on both sides by steep mountains, dark and foreboding. As Romano walked the canyon faces carved into the hard rock leapt out at him.

At the end of the canyon stood a man with a deathly appearance, Romano recognized him as Goodman, the condemned man.

"Its alright." Goodman assured him. "Your time will come."

The condemned man's head turned to face him. Smiling serenely at Romano, he said. "Governor, you are a man with a conscience, a strong man. Why wouldn't you save me? Cowardice is the greatest sin."

"I don't know, I don't know," said the sleeping Governor.

The governor's dream was interrupted that day by the voice of his secretary whispering,

"Sir, sir."

Half asleep, Romano sat up and asked.

"Is it done? Have they killed him?"

The secretary was a little taken a back and moved away from the governor whose face had now taken on a terrible expression.

Walking to his desk, still half asleep, the Governor picked up a red ball point pen and signed the death warrants hastily.

It was a ten minute drive to the prison from the governor's mansion. The sky had darkened considerably during the early evening and a severe thunderstorm threat had been issued.

The prison was situated outside the city limits on a small hill, where it stood ominously overlooking the town below.

Sitting in the rear seat of the governor's limousine, Romano gazed out at the neat streets. What a beautiful city, he thought. So tidy and clean.

It was Governor Romano's first visit to an execution chamber, and he did not care for it. It smelt uncannily clean, almost septic, and Romano was reminded of a hospital he had once had an operation in.

On his way through the hallway that joined the condemned cell to the execution chamber, the Governor met Warden Thomas.

"Everything ready?" asked Romano.

"Yes sir," answered the Warden.

"Is he sedated?" asked Romano.

"No," answered the Warden. "He refused sedatives."

"What?" asked Romano and incredulous look on his face.

"He said he wished to die with a clear mind."

Romano winced.

"Give the man sedatives now," he ordered.

"Too late." snapped the Warden.

The witness chamber contained few people. Three rows of seats each five deep. Romano saw the speaker, the attorney general and several other members of the legislature. Scanning the room he noticed an older woman sat in the back row crying.

The condemned man lay strapped to the gurney, his hands and feet bound crucifixion style. To his right stood the warden his blank expression reflecting the somber atmosphere.

At the back of the chamber, two burly guards stood exchanging jokes.

Strapped to the gurney, Goodman remained silent. As the moment approached, the executioner swiveled the gurney round to make the prisoner's legs face his witnesses. Then, pressing a lever with his foot, he tilted the gurney to an upright position.

The spread-eagled Goodman was addresses by the Warden.

"Simon Goodman, do you have anything to say before sentence is passed?"

Goodman smiled at the people assembled in the chamber.

Turning to Romano, Goodman said, "Goodbye Governor, until we meet again."

Romano's face drained.

Romano looked slowly at the telephone on the execution chamber's wall and then turned to see the firm gaze of the speaker staring right at him. The governor closed his eyes.......

In that short moment the governor imagined the telephone ringing. The warden stepped across slowly to answer it. Hurry up, man, urged the governor. Nodding his head and speaking into the phone the Warden directed the guards to unstrapp the bound prisoner who sat up smiling at the relieved Governor.

Romano opened his eyes. The condemned man now lat flat on his gurney, his eyes fixed intently on the execution chamber's ceiling.

Within ten minutes, the prison doctor pronounced Goodman dead, and the witnesses rose silently and headed toward the door. The older lady who had been crying in the back row walked toward the motionless governor and stopped opposite him.

"He was a good boy. No matter what they say, he meant well."

The governor a man used to controlling his emotions and thoughts said. "I know he was."

Then, touching the old woman on the shoulder, he directed out of the witness room.

As Romano left the execution chamber the fast moving storm was right over the prison. Thunderclaps echoed down the hallways and the sound of rain on the roof made all else inaudible. Passing by the reception desk, Romano waited on account of the torrential downfall. The officer on duty acknowledged him, and they shared a short conversation on the severity of the storm.

"They say the state house has been struck by lightening," remarked the officer.

The Governor nodded.

Romano glanced around the reception area. The walls were bare with the exception of a large clock on the wall behind the receptionist's desk.

As the rain eased, Romano waved through the glass door to his waiting driver. Stepping nimbly to avoid the puddles, he exited the prison. As he did the clock on the wall struck midnight.

Thus Pat Romano fifth Libertarian Governor of Florida met the morning after Good Friday.

The Meanest Church in England

Taking Loddarts Lane east toward Wycke Hill, one passes through what was once the center of the village of Hazeleigh. This decaying village, once its own parish, has now been incorporated into Woodham Mortimer, a larger one abutting its western boundary.

Old Hazeleigh was built around Loddarts Hill, which served as the centre providing an excellent view over the surrounding flatlands, a perfect defense against marauders.

It is a short, sharp, unmemorable climb up the western slope of the hill, but on the eastern side the descent is long and picturesque, affording the traveler an excellent view of the western approaches to Maldon, the next town over.

During the descent, if one turns off Loddarts Lane on Mill Lane in the direction of the Old Hall, one is brought to the edge of Hazeleigh woods, whose chief claim to fame is housing the remains of the meanest church in England. This is its story.

The rude wood structure to St Nicholas was erected in a clearing in the center of Hazeleigh wood sometime in the fifteenth century by locals in the employ of the local squire. The squire, who resided in the Old Hall and owned the wood, put the church together cheaply, but with good intention, so the villagers would not have to walk the considerable distance to Woodham Mortimer to worship.

The building a small weatherboard affair, no more than fifty feet square had little of architectural interest to offer, the short pitched roof, gutter less and leaky running the length of the church. A crude belfry had been added in the 17th century, the workmanship so poor that it was considered unsafe even then for a bell, a solitary cross on its roof being the only sign to identify it as a place of worship

In his haste, or maybe his desire to be frugal, the squire had neglected to purchase any glass for the two windows and they were left as open holes. After a couple of years of damp seats and howling winds the parishioners had boarded the holes. Being a ramshackle affair, it had difficulty attracting a priest, until one summer the young rector of an adjoining parish was persuaded to hold a weekly service.

The church was no bigger than a small schoolhouse with roughly hewn pews and a dirt floor. In winter it was punishingly cold and in summer stiflingly hot. The attendees were mainly employees of the squire and resided in tithe cottages dotted further up Mill Lane. The church went on this way for two centuries until the late 1800's, when an event took place which was to hasten its demise.

By this time, the church had a regular attendance of some twenty five souls. The rector was still from the adjoining village, but by now, as well the Sunday service he officiated over weddings and funerals.

A large graveyard had grown up around the church which still lay hidden in the woods and still had no windows. It may well have continued this way had not the present Squire realized that the land and church built on it belonged to him.

The squire, whose name was De Greywater, was an affable fellow and much concerned with the responsibilities of his position. Upon finding he owned the church, he offered for a small sum to cover transfer taxes to sell it to the Bishopric of Chelmsford. This he imparted to the present rector whose name was Sheppard and with this in mind they visited the Bishop in Chelmsford.

Bishop Laidler, a stalwart of the Anglican faith was much amused when he heard the story, saying he saw no impediment to an agreement and put his clerk on it immediately.

If only things had been that easy.

The bishop's clerk was a diligent young fellow by the name of Joyce. He got to work on the deed immediately. In those days things took some time, so it was a few months later that the recorder's office replied with a letter stating that no such church existed. This did not surprise the clerk; a lot of older buildings were not recorded. So, he proceeded to the district lists. Oddly enough the church was not recorded there either. Frustrated, he sent for a surveyor and ordered a full survey of the property.

The bishop meanwhile inquired of the rector how long he had been giving services, and if would he continue. The rector, an employee of an obscure Oxford college whiling out his years in the Essex countryside, stated that his predecessor had informed him that it was his theological and civil duty to administer to these poor folk and so he would continue as needed, his parish had been doing it for two hundred years and he saw no reason to discontinue the tradition.

The rector added that the parishioners were an odd lot; they tended to keep to themselves, most of the service they conducted themselves in Latin, an odd thing, asking only that he bless the congregation at the end. Burials, which were few and far between, were also very private affairs.

Bishop Laidler's interest was piqued and he asked whether he could attend a service, which the rector discouraged, and recounting tales of the church's filth, stench and infrequency of services. The bishop then inquired as to the legend about the lack of windows, adding that Christ could hardly be expected to look in on his flock with an opening. The rector replied he had no idea why it was windowless, but the Lord was all-seeing and all- knowing; windows did not apply to him.

Believing that the rector was directing his attention elsewhere and unsure of the theological implications of a church with now official rector in residence Bishop Laidler made a mental note to look in on the church.

Some six months hence, the Bishop alighted from a carriage at the old hall. The squire had invited him to visit in order that he should view the church he was to acquire. After pleasantries and a nice late lunch, the bishop and his clerk Joyce followed the squire down Mill Lane into the woods.

No wonder, thought the Bishop, that this place was forgotten. From the edge of the wood only a small path was visible. He could not believe there was a building back in there. The three men walked back into the wood for a good five minutes until they came upon the wooden structure.

It was totally surrounded with gravestones, many falling apart as was the building itself. The weatherboarding was rotted, much of it eaten away by grubs and splattered with deep green lichen, the entrance was a large oak door with nails dotted all over it. The solitary cross still stood atop the pigeon-filled belfry, the only thing that distinguished the building from a common farm shack.

When the three ventured inside, they found an empty room with a dirt floor. The pews were large benches evidently knocked together many years ago and there was a crude altar at the far end.

"This is awful," exclaimed the Bishop, brushing a spider from his jacket. He envisioned what must be done.

"This place must be razed," he said. "And a new stone building will be put up with stained-glass windows and a decent altar for these poor people to pray at."

At that moment, the squire pulled Laidler's sleeve.

"I believe there will be short service the evening, Your Grace," he said.

"Well, let's wait," replied the bishop.

"It would perhaps be wise to secret ourselves," chimed in the clerk.

The three men moved cautiously outside, deciding after some discussion to hide themselves in a ditch some ten yards from the church. The ditch, messy and home to a myriad of horse flies was very uncomfortable.

In time, about twelve people appeared walking silently in single file along the forest path. They were joined by Rector Sheppard, his black cassock brushing the undergrowth. The group went inside the church and closed the door behind them.

Hidden in the ditch, the three onlookers waited patiently for something to happen.

The bishop, surprisingly agile for a man his age, moved closer to the church when he saw all was clear. From the sound of it, the service had already started. Arriving at the building, he peeped in through a crack in the weatherboard.

The rector was sitting down on a pew reading silently while the rest of the congregation was being led by an older man in farm laborer's clothes. The man spoke in clear liturgical Latin; the bishop, a long time out of academia, took a little time to comprehend what was going on. Once he did, he rose quickly, ran around the church wall to the front door and burst in, knocking the rotten wooden door off its hinges. The congregation was astounded. The rector leaped to his feet, dropping his bible. The laborer who was leading the service put his cap back on his head. The last Roman Catholic mass in pure middle-Latin had been interrupted.

The bishop said nothing at first. Then, after some thought, he crossed himself and took his leave.

The congregants, after getting over the initial shock, continued unperturbed. The walk back to the old hall was a somber one, neither bishop nor companions having much to say to each other. Taking his leave of the squire, the bishop, hurried back to Chelmsford, muddied and bemused.

The following day, the bishop called upon the rector. The conversation was congenial, although the bishop's points were made with the utmost severity.

"This cannot continue," he said.

"I know," replied the Rector. "But it has for several hundred years; my predecessor did not know what to do either."

"All these years these people have been worshipping this way under the auspices of the Anglican church?" inquired Bishop Laidler.

"Yes," replied the Rector.

"They say," said the Bishop, "that it's called the meanest church in England."

"Yes," replied the Rector. "Most people assume it's because of the lack of windows, but that was just for privacy. It's really because there has never been a collection plate!"

The bishop grinned. It was the grin of a man who had just found his life's cause.

The rest is history. The small wooden church in Hazeleigh wood was condemned and torn down. Some of the foundation and a number of gravestones have survived and are still visible to this day. The congregation was encouraged to worship at a newer church off the main Burnham road.

It is the opinion of most local scholars that they were absorbed into the Anglican faith over the next generation and soon forgot the ways in which they had been raised. In the census of 1978 Hazeleigh was listed as having no inhabitants who identified themselves as Roman Catholic.

Tish and Tosh's Curtain Call

Albert Pierrepoint, dressed in a black serge suit, caught an earlier tram than usual that Tuesday morning. The conductor, a white-haired fellow with a cigarette in his mouth and tatty uniform on his back knew Albert and was quick with a quip.

"Who's got a date with the devil today?"

"I have," snapped Albert with irritation.

The conductor, a little surprised at the demeanor of his normally good natured passenger, made to retort back, but thought better of it. Without further conversation he clipped Albert's ticket and moved on down the aisle.

Albert had never thought too deeply about his second profession, proffering to describe it as "a living" to anyone who asked. He had however in the last few years gained a certain level of notoriety. After his work with the war office his name had become more recognizable, Albert detested the new found infamy.

Today, however, was different. The man he was to execute was known to him. In fact he could almost be called a friend. Staring out of the tram window into the misty Manchester morning Albert's mind drifted back to a night some years ago when the troubadour he called Tish had first come into his pub, "The Poor Struggler." It had been a cold November evening with a touch of frost in the air....

It was a cold November evening with a touch of frost in the air. The fireplace in the saloon bar of "The Poor Struggler" was ablaze and a full crowd was expected. The publican Albert Pierrepoint was already busy serving, his regulars having arrived earlier than usual, keen to appreciate the fire and spend their weekly earnings. Albert was a good host, attentive to his clients' needs and firm but polite if they got out of hand. The pub he and his wife Grace had run for the past five years was small affair, slotted into the row of terraced houses which straddled one of Oldham's working class neighborhoods. The pub had provided Albert with a decent living, and its name was his own grim joke and his second profession.

Albert and Grace were popular in the neighborhood and trade had steadily grown over the years they had owned the bar. To add to the weekend merriment, Albert had introduced a small piano to the saloon area. Weekend nights became full of song and dance until last orders were called.

That night, a young Mancunian named Jim came in midway through the evening, tall and slim with the good looks that women often find attractive. He sat on a bar stool and quietly drank his beer. Later, when the piano player started up, Jim moved over to join the group who had started to sing and joined in, a smile on his face.

When the pianist launched into "Danny Boy," Jim started singing the first verse. The regulars, impressed by his perfect pitch, had remained silent. By the second verse, Albert, returning from the public bar, had come across and joined Jim. Both men had good voices and, when finished, smiled admiringly at each other while the patrons male and female applauded them.

"Thanks, Tosh," said Jim.

"Aye, Tish," replied Albert and a local legend was born.

After that night Jim became a regular in "The Poor Struggler." His duet with the infamous publican became a Friday night draw and Jim's good looks helped attract more young women to the previously male dominated establishment.

Jim Corbett had been married, but his wife, tired of his philandering, had thrown him out, allowing him only scant visitation with his eleven-year-old son. Jim, however, refused to learn his lesson, and his reputation as a ladies' man spread through the neighborhood.

One night, two young girls, barely twenty in age, escorted by a young man came in for a drink. Jim sat at the bar and was besotted. Asking the girl, whose name was Eliza, out on a date the following night, she acquiesced, and within a week they were a couple, spending every Friday and Saturday in Albert's Oldham pub.

Walking the short distance between his tram stop and Strangeways Prison, Albert thought through his morning. The condemned man Jim Corbett had in lieu of a last visit from his brother asked to meet his executioner in person, an event Albert was trying to avoid.

Strangeways Prison is a grim looking Victorian building, exuding an aura of doom and gloom, a remnant of the days when prisons were made to look dreadful to deter the local populace. Approaching the main gate, Albert noticed details about Strangeways he had passed over in these past twenty years. People crossed the road to avoid the place, giving it an unlucky stare. As Albert arrived at the front gate, the guard motioned him into to the admitting area. The mist was lifting slightly and Albert grimaced to himself.

The mist had lifted on the Saturday night that Albert had last seen Jim. Coming to the pub punctually at eight Jim had appeared somewhat preoccupied. Albert knew of his marital troubles and tried perking him up.

"Hey up, Tish, what you havin'?" he asked

"Usual Tosh," replied Jim, a touch of melancholy in his voice.

Albert was used to listening to customers' troubles, but Jim always seemed so jovial. He could not imagine his friend having any worries. Pulling his friend a pint of ale he put it on the counter before him.

"Wife still after you lad?" he asked. When Jim offered Albert money, the publican shook his head.

"This one's on me Tish," he said

"Me wife hates me. It's me gal," said Jim raising his glass in a toast to his host. "She says she loves me, but I think she seeing another."

Albert had been a publican many years and knew better than to intervene in personal matters, plus Eliza did not have a good reputation around his area.

"Don't fret Tish, there's plenty more where she come from."

Jim just nodded, his lips touching his pint glass. Taking at pack of cigarettes from his jacket pocket, he lit one.

"Cheer up Tish, wait while we get singing," continued Albert

"Landlord, if you please," a voice from down the long wooden bar was calling for service, the empty glass pushed to the serving edge of the bar. Albert left Jim sat by the bar and went about his job.

That Saturday continued as usual. When ten o'clock, struck the pianist started to play a string of favorites on the piano. "Mother Kelly's doorstep," "I've got sixpence," and many others. The crowd sat down at the neat tables and began singing along as normal, hands clapping in rhythm with the melodies.

Later the pianist started into "Danny Boy." As he did, Jim's girl Eliza opened the saloon bar door and walked in. Jim looked over, pleased to see her, and winked, his red face shining in the light. Albert started into the second verse of "Danny Boy" and Jim, eyes closed ,hummed along, his arm around the publican's shoulders.

After time was called, the patrons slowly drank their final drinks and exited into the cold night air. Sat at the bar Jim, very drunk held Eliza's hand as he gazed into her eyes.

"Come on, Tish, lad," said Albert, walking over and touching his singing partners arm.

"Alright, alright, " replied Jim. "I'm leaving Tosh, I'm leaving."

Helping Eliza on with her jacket he winked at Albert. Albert smiled back. Old Tish certainly had a way with the women.

"We're going' to a hotel in Ashton," said Jim. "And tomorrow we're going to get engaged."

"Congratulations, Tish, " replied the publican half in jest. "Be sure to send me a wedding invite," he giggled.

Jim and Eliza staggered to the door; Albert held it open and said he would see them both tomorrow night.

Neither crossed "The Poor Struggler" threshold ever again.

Albert was nervous as he climbed the metal staircase to the condemned cell. His footsteps echoed along the landing mixing tunefully with the keys which hung rattling from the warden's belt. The walk along the landing was painful for Albert. He heard every footstep, and his eyes caught every shape.

The warden stopped outside the condemned mans cell, thrusting his hands into his pockets he asked. "Are you sure you want to do this Mr. Pierrepoint?"

Albert nodded solemnly. The door opened cleanly and they walked in.

Sat on a plain wrought iron bed was Jim Corbett, sallow and pale, his frightened eyes sunk far into his face. Gone was the smiling troubadour Albert remembered. The man who looked up at him that day was already dead.

Albert, removing his trilby hat and motioning for the warden and guards to leave, sat down on the bed next to Jim.

"Hello, Tish," he said.

"Hello, Tosh," Jim replied.

"You wanted to see me lad?" asked Albert after a short silence.

"I just wanted to say goodbye proper-like, so you knew there's no hard feelings." said Jim.

"Tell me you didn't Tish, tell me they're wrong." Albert looked pleadingly at his singing partner.

"Tell me you didn't croak her." Gone was the orderly directness of the executioner, now Albert spoke as he would serve his friend on a Saturday night...

Jim looked his friend straight in the eye. Albert read the answer.

"I was drunk Tosh, you know I was lad. You served me."

"Aye, Tish but you'd no need drinking more and croakin' 'er."

Silence reigned for what seemed like forever, before Albert asked."Why did you want to see me, Tish?"

Jim Corbett looked his old friend in the eye,

"I 'ave a last request. An since what I done to Eliza that night I don't fancy drinking no more. Me wife won't bring me boy to see me. I hear she's taken up with a sailor."

"So," asked Albert

"It won't hurt none Tosh will it, the 'angin' I mean." Jim looked down at his manacled hands.

"No," said Albert truthfully. "It's quick."

"I'm glad," said Jim.

"Glad?" asked Albert.

"Glad, it's me mate what's 'angin' me Tosh."

Albert said nothing. He had lost his tongue.

"Can we sing it then Tosh lad, one more time for old time's sake? Let's sing Danny Boy."

"Aye, Tish, that I can."

The sound of two baritones singing a duet was a first for the condemned cell. The only audience was the officer on duty and the hangman's assistant checking the gallows. The mournful Irish air floated down the corridor as the executioner and his victim sought absolution.

On his way down from the condemned cell, Albert stopped to check the arrangements on the gallows. His assistant, a silent, stoic Yorkshire man named Harry, informed him that all was ready.

"Well Harry," said Albert, "I think you can pull the lever on this one."

Before Harry had chance to ask why, Albert had left the room, and all he heard were the echo of his footsteps as he walked down the landing.

The execution proceedings began three hours later. Albert once again entered the condemned cell, this time in the company of two burly prison guards and a chaplin. Immediately they entered the cell, the guards made to restrain Jim, but Albert with a depth of voice rarely heard in one his size said sharply. "Stop, now. He's not gonna give us any trouble. Are you Tish, lad?"

"No, Tosh," replied the condemned man.

It is a short walk to the gallows, although to both Albert and Jim it seemed like an eternity that day. The chaplin murmured a benediction as Jim was led to the chalked square on the trap door. A hood was put quickly over his head and the noose lowered and tightened.

Stepping back, Albert Pierrepoint signaled to his assistant to pull the trap door release. Within three seconds Jim Corbett was dead.

That night at "The Poor Struggler," Albert, despondent after the days events and the worse for drink, got into an argument with a stranger from a national newspaper about capital punishment, the stranger implied that deterrence was the greatest weapon against capital crime, and he got the full brunt of Albert's wrath.

"I just hanged an ordinary man, his crime weren't premeditated, and he just lost his temper. This man knew who I was, what I did and what could 'appen to 'im. We sang songs together at that piano over there the night he croaked his gal. This job of mine ain't a deterrent. It's murder, bloody murder."

To see the usually reticent publican so aroused upset the locals, and they asked the stranger to leave.

Albert Pierrepont went about his duties more solemnly after that November day in 1954. Gone was the impish grin which had brought him so much notoriety. The man who hanged some of the century's most bloodthirsty killers and half the Nazi hierarchy at Nuremburg was a shadow of his former self for several years hence, eventually leaving his infamous profession over a supposed financial dispute. But those of us who remember him the evening after he hanged Tish came to a far different conclusion.

Stille Nacht, a Mousical

Joseph was an orderly man and during the festive season was no different. The week before the Christingle service, he had ordered a massive clean-out of the church. The belfry, apse and nave were to be spotlessly clean, he told his staff. The rector intended to enter this most solemn of seasons, physically and spiritually clean. He had brought in new supplies from Bremen in order to accomplish his task.

The day the supplies were delivered, Joseph engaged the services of a young man from a neighboring village. The fellow was considered somewhat simple-minded and unfit for general employ. Joseph had, at the request of the boy's father, found meaningful work for him with the rest of the church janitorial staff.

The young man, Rudolf had an affinity for animals; he had in fact spent most of his life caring for the animals who were attracted to his father's farm-house during the winter months. After many lectures to his simple-minded son had failed, his father decided to use poison on the collection of rodents and varmints that had taken up residence around his house. Not wishing to hurt his son physically or spiritually he had arranged for his temporary removal to Joseph's church staff.

The church was medieval in design. The walls were made of thick stone with a bell-tower at the rear end beyond the altar. The tower housed two large bells that were rung before each service by Joseph and the organist, Franz Gruber. The exterior of the church had been plaster-finished and white-washed, although it was in a state of disrepair. The interior had fared a little better, although under Joseph's meter and had been somewhat restored. It boasted to its credit some of the finest stained glass in Wutternburg. The nave windows in particular had glorious versions of the adoration of the magi and the pieta.

Although stunning, the interior was, however, dusty and dirty. Collections of dust and leaves had blown through the door on service days and, with the debris came insects and mice. Joseph was not totally sure when the mouse problem had begun, but it had got out of control. He had tried poison, but that had failed. He bought a cat, but the creature found the church too cold and damp, preferring to spend her evenings by the rectory fire rather than catching mice. The last straw had been some crude mechanical traps. After catching his fingers and those of the verger on several occasions Joseph decided only a good clean-out would work.

During this time, Joseph had become a slight mousophobe and kept at least the vestry very clean. Due to his heavy work load around advent, Joseph left the cleaning of the church to Rudolf this year.

Rudolf went about his task with due vigor and within the first several days had swept and wiped the area from the great organ at the base of the belfry to the altar. The Rector himself having cleaned behind the altar, all that remained was to clean the bell-tower.

The tower was small and inaccessible except from directly under the bell. The stairs had rotted many years ago, and access was only afforded by a ladder. Rudolf carried the ladder over from the vicarage on this particular morning. Stopping along the gravel pathway which led up to the front door of church, the amiable laborer took in the morning air. Standing still he watched two song birds playing in an oak tree. Rudolf had always been tuned into nature, and his keen senses caught every move in the birds' parade.

Leaving the morning behind him, he headed into the church. Placing his ladder against the rafter above the bells, he gingerly climbed up. When he was abreast the bells, he stopped. On a ledge cut into the tower wall was wooden box without a lid, obviously the remnant of renovation work some years previously. Balancing himself with his foot on the top of bell case, Rudolf took the box under his arm and peered in curiously. A family of mice had nested inside the box. The fur and droppings produced an acrid smell. Rudolf did not initially realize that by removing the box he had also removed the mice's way in and out. Taking the box, he descended the ladder.

Rudolf was a kindly fellow and he found on closer examination that the mother mouse had already given birth. The furless mouse babies lay cowering in the box corner under their mother. His protective spirit aroused, Rudolf started thinking of some place to secrete the box. Many ideas came to him but he settled on a small area beneath the organ. There, he reasoned, it was warm, dry and somewhat sheltered and would allow the animals to come and go from the box by using the bellow arms. He pushed the box far underneath, and for good measure took some bread from his lunch and slid it in after the box. After this, he continued with the cleaning of the belfry.

For a week, Rudolf went into the church on his lunch break, ostensibly to pray, but always taking with him a crust of bread which he left in the opening beneath the organ.

In preparation for Christmas, Joseph had written a poem, which with the help of Franz he started to put to music. Joseph thought it captured the mood of the moment, somewhat solemn and slow, but with its own meaningful cheer underneath. Joseph had named his hymn, "The son of God is born."

He met Franz each day after dinner in the church to practice. As the week went on however practice however became difficult. The organ was beginning to sound cranky. Joseph put this down to age and dampness. He reminded the Bishop in a letter that week that singing was an essential part of his ministry and a replacement organ a necessity.

As Christmas approached, the organ became worse and Joseph and Franz began to worry about their Christmas Eve service's entertainment. After having his verger examine the instrument to no avail, Joseph sent to the next town for the organ specialist. A message came back the following day that the man was busy and could not come until after the holiday.

Franz let it be known to the vicar that he was unwilling to play the instrument should it get any worse. But worse it got. On Christmas Eve the organ simply scratched.

Joseph was dismayed. A Christmas service without music..., the thought upset the timid rector.

On Christmas Eve morning the rector awoke. He had gone to sleep thinking and on waking thought he had a solution. Quickly dressing, he ran to Franz's house. The organist was surprised to see the rector so early, but nevertheless invited him in.

Sitting down at the table and refusing refreshment, Joseph said that he remembered that Franz played the guitar. Tonight, he said, in honor of the birth of our Lord, the mass would include guitar music. Franz was unsure. This was a solemn occasion and he did not know how the locals would take to him playing a guitar. Joseph reassured him that everything would be fine.

On Christmas Eve, at eleven o'clock the locals walked into the candlelit church for the midnight mass, some having walked quite a distance. Before long most of the pews were filled, and only standing room was left. On their way in each parishioner had been given a song sheet and there was a dull murmur within the nave as they waited for the organ to signal the beginning of the service.

When the rector hurried out from the vestry to the pulpit and announced that evening's accompaniment would be on the guitar, there was a groan and then some muttering. Finally a jovial member of the congregation started to clap and stamp. The others suitably loosened by intakes of alcohol also began to stamp and yell.

The commotion sent the already petrified mice scurrying from under the organ running down the nave. This excited several of the women who screamed in horror. The high pitch screams mingled with tramping caused Franz's guitar to fall off its perch on to a pew and split at the neck.

When Franz and Joseph saw what had happened, they and several others chased after the poor rodents driving them ultimately back under the organ. There they sat atop the bellow sleeve frightened for their lives.

Joseph was beside himself and Franz, frustrated, leant one hand upon the organ keys.

The organ omitted a long mournful sound which echoed throughout the church. When he heard the sound Joseph looked quizzically at his organist.

"May be the planks are warped?" asked the rector.

"It's not possible," replied the bemused organist playing another couple of keys. Each was long and mournful.

Not wanting to risk being embarrassed, Joseph asked Franz to play a short carol they had composed a year or so earlier.

Starting the melody, Franz played as delicately as possible, his thin fingers sliding slowly over the keys. In the church, sudden silence descended. The parishioners soon forgot about the earlier incident. The vicar led the church in song, and underneath the organ a family of scared mice clung for dear life to the shredded bellow sheave as the trapped air exited between their tiny legs.

Years hence, the baby mice, now fully grown, had left their nest and found mates of their own. The simple-minded youth employed by the diocese that winter had returned to his family and married. Joseph and Franz however bickered on for many a silent night about the tune they had written.